MY BLIND DATE IS A ZOMBIE

MY BLIND DATE IS A ZOMBIE

A PARANORMAL ROMANCE

LOVE IS BLIND
BOOK FOUR

DAPHNE BLOOM

Red Empress Publishing
www.RedEmpressPublishing.com

Cover by Cherith Vaughan
Facebook.com/CoversbyCherith

CHAPTER 1

The bloody rats were at it again. Letting out a groan of frustration, I sat up on the bed and grabbed one of my smaller pillows, chucking it at the ceiling as if it would do any good. The pillow fell uselessly and lamely with a muted thud to the floor while the little monsters nesting in my ceiling kept running around as if it was the bloody Olympics, disturbing my beauty sleep for the third flipping night in a row.

I wouldn't have minded if I hadn't just come from a packed club, my ears still ringing from all the loud music, feet and back aching, and a hangover already building. And this was after spending half the day teaching a bunch of rowdy eight-year-olds how to paint with watercolors. But I suppose that was what I got for leasing a dingy apartment in the sketchiest part of town instead of just swallowing my pride and agreeing to let my parents rent a proper apartment for me. But I didn't want all the rules and conditions that came with a swanky loft apartment on Rain Avenue.

No way! I was perfectly fine in my rat-infested apartment. Even if the little buggers did leave their droppings everywhere, including in the cereal box. Even if they ate through almost all of my clothes. Even if I was sure they were watching me all the time. Just watching…

Still, I'd paid for all of this myself. And with my savings steadily building up, I would be able to afford a much better place in no time. For the time being, I just had to twist my landlord's arm to do something about my rat problem—literally twist his arm if he kept giving me the runaround. Or convince him to allow me to release a rat snake since none of the mouse traps or rat poison I put out was working.

Giving up on getting any more sleep, at least until the rats in my ceiling quieted down, I threw on a robe over my Harry Potter-themed PJs and went in search of some warm milk.

"And of course, there would be none," I muttered grumpily, staring blankly into my empty fridge, the light burning my retinas. Aside from a block of cheese and left-over Chinese takeout, all I had was a half-empty bottle of Jack Daniels. That would work as a sedative too, I supposed. And you know what else would help lull me to sleep? Drawing.

I didn't currently have a commission piece in the works, having delivered the last one the day before. I was taking two days to let my brain reset before moving on to my next order. But for as long as I could remember, I had always been working on a bunch of different graphic novel ideas. None of them had ever made it beyond the first couple of chapters, instead collecting dust in my digital folders because Imposter Syndrome sucks and I didn't think I had the storytelling skills to support the awesome artwork. But, hey, a girl can dream, can't she?

The one I was working on at the moment—cleverly

named *Idea #75*—was an adventure fantasy that revolved around a shy, time-traveling librarian and a magic sword-wielding, broody knight-slash-sorcerer. Perching myself at my workstation, I took a swig of the Jack Daniels and called up the digital app I used for drawing on my iPad and lost myself in the process.

I barely noticed the sky lightening outside the window as the sun peeked over the horizon and bathed Mystic Cove in its golden glow. I was far too focused on the strokes of my stylus pen on the tablet, on getting the frown wrinkles on my grumpy hero just right—and the sexy swoop of his hair too.

Ever since I walked into my first art class at age six, I could get lost in painting or drawing for hours on end without coming up for air, until my fingers cramped up or my vision started to blur and my back throbbed. Much to my parents' dismay, art was my life, my soul. Dear Mom and Dad had meant for it to be nothing more than a hobby they could brag about to their friends at the local country club. I sucked at violin and piano and did not have the patience or grace needed for ballet or horseback riding, so art lessons were their last attempt, and I had taken to it like a duck to water. So much so that instead of getting the fancy MBA they had planned out for me since before I was an actual fetus, I went ahead and graduated with a bachelor's in fine arts.

Unfortunately, the only job such a degree had afforded me was teaching the next generation of dreamers with no real idea of what to do with myself. Now, I was living on the side of town Rebecca and Daniel Flowers would never dare to step their Louboutin-clad feet in. Living the dream, indeed.

~*~

The blare of my phone alarm startled me out of my flow state. It felt like waking up from a different kind of sleep. My back creaked and groaned from being hunched over for so long and my eyes burned when I blinked.

Friday through Sunday, I taught art classes to kids at High Tide, the local gallery and art school. It wasn't supposed to be a permanent position, but the owner, Landon Grayson, has been intimating that it might become a full-time thing. The problem was that I wasn't sure teaching art was what I wanted to do with my life. But I also didn't want to work full-time at the bookstore I part-timed at. As much as I loved getting discounts on all my favorite thrillers, romances, and comic books, I just couldn't picture myself working there past my mid-twenties. So much for all those career fairs and guidance and counseling meetings in college because they'd done jack-all in preparing me for adulthood. I'd just turned twenty-three, but I still felt like a clueless sixteen-year-old most of the time. I was working to pay the bills, but I didn't have a career. I felt aimless.

It was only when I was about to take a shower that I remembered that Sunday's art lessons had been canceled due to some minor renovation work at the gallery, so I could have completely ignored the 7 a.m. wake-up call and slept in. I dragged myself back to my bed and curled up, ready to zonk out, at least until it was time to prepare for the monthly family Sunday brunch at The Black Pearl. I would have enjoyed nothing more than staying in and licking my wounds, recuperating from the last week, maybe picking up some groceries later in the day, but Mother would eviscerate me if I missed family brunch.

As if just by thinking it, I sent the thought out into the universe and directly to my mother's phone. The custom ringtone I'd assigned to her—a remix of the *Jaws* theme song —roused me out of a deep sleep with a start. I didn't even realize I'd fallen asleep. I wiped the drool from the side of my mouth as I blindly reached for my phone on the nightstand.

"'Lo?" I answered, my voice groggy and heavy from sleep. The first word out of my mother's mouth was an exasperated curse.

"Dianna Flowers, please don't tell me that you're still in bed at—" There was a short pause as she likely checked the time on the pretty little rose gold watch Dad got her for their thirty-fifth wedding anniversary. "—eleven-fifteen in the morning. I just knew that if I didn't call you to remind you about the brunch, you'd probably miss it."

"I wasn't going to miss it, Mom. You've reminded me about it like a thousand times this week alone. And when have I ever missed a family brunch when I was in town?" I flopped onto my back and stared at the ceiling, waiting for her reply.

"Fair point. I just wanted to let you know that I am sending your brother to pick you up. My heart can't take you driving all the way to The Black Pearl on that safety hazard of yours," she bemoaned, referring to my totally rad black and purple scooter.

"Dion or James?" I asked, crossing my fingers that it wasn't the latter. I loved my oldest brother James, but ever since he got promoted to junior partner at his law firm, he'd turned into a duplicate of our father. I did not want to spend any amount of time with him in a small, enclosed space and listen to him lecture me about my poor life choices or offer to find me a respectable job.

"Dion. Jamie will be bringing a lady friend to the brunch to introduce her to the family. I trust that you will be on your best behavior. And for the love of Pete, no talk of whatever weird and disturbing fad you're into these days."

I ignored the jab, far more interested in the fact that my

perpetual bachelor of a brother who went through women like cheap shoes was bringing someone to introduce to the folks. "Is he trying to scare her away? If this girl were a keeper, Jamie would at least wait to introduce her to Dion and me."

My mother snorted at the comment. My brother Dion, who was a year younger than me, was the "black sheep" of the family, even blacker than me. Most of the time, our family was too embarrassed to be seen with us in public, and we were a source of constant disappointment to our father, who had hoped to see us working more prestigious and high-rolling jobs.

I ended the call and rushed to get ready. I didn't have a lot of fancy brunch dresses lying around, so I chose a vintage, spaghetti-strapped, V-necked, 50s-style housedress with little cartoonish suns and crescent moons printed all over it. Because I knew Dad and my grandfather would gripe about showing my cleavage, I added a long-sleeved black mesh top underneath. It was sheer but still better than nothing.

A little blush, some thick eyeliner, and matte, dark purple lipstick completed the look. I went easy on my piercings this time around, heeding my mother's warning to dress appropriately. Aside from the tongue piercing, nose stud, and hoop above my belly button, I wore two fake amethyst hoops on my eyebrow. I had four other piercings along the shells of both my ears, and most days I wore either studs or rings in all of them, but I gave them a pass for the moment.

My phone vibrated on the counter, Dion letting me know that he was waiting for me downstairs. I quickly pulled on my thigh-high lace socks and Doc Martens boots, grabbed my bag, and ran out the door.

~*~

The Black Pearl was located on the promenade overlooking the beach and was just as busy as it usually was during the height of tourist season in winter. The hostess greeted my brother and me by name and led us to the mezzanine floor, where our family was seated for privacy.

"You ready for this?" Dion asked under his breath when we cleared the stairs and spotted Dad's head of golden honey-blond hair, hair that all his children, except Juno, our seventeen-year-old sister, inherited. She and Mom were both strawberry blondes.

"Nope. But maybe he'll be too distracted by Jamie's girlfriend to lay into use. He's always on his best behavior when guests are around," I replied, pasting a smile on my face when Granddad spotted Dion and me and broke out in a wide smile, waving us over.

"One can only hope," Dion mumbled miserably, hand on my lower back as he led me to the table.

A round of greetings that involved a lot of hugging and cheek kissing went around the table. It felt like the whole family had shown up for Sunday brunch, including all three of our grandparents and our Uncle Hank, who was the mayor of Mystic Cove. All the Flowers siblings were present, except for Mirabelle, my older sister, who was getting her doctorate in psychology in Germany. Jamie's girlfriend, Sally, appeared overwhelmed by the lot of us.

I was seated between her and Juno, who'd grunted a greeting and went back to staring at her phone screen the second everyone was seated despite our mother hissing at her to put it away.

I leaned over and whispered to Sally, who was staring wide-eyed at the heated debate between my brothers, Dad, Uncle Hank, and both granddads over a football game. "No one will judge you for ordering a stronger drink, you know.

Except for Juno, none of us ever make it out of any of these gatherings without knocking back a drink or two,"

"That's what you think," Juno scoffed. She thought I didn't know that she slipped a couple of bucks to whoever served us to slip champagne into her orange juice.

"Even your grandfather?" Sally whispered back, her gaze fixated on granddad's clerical collar, our father's father.

"Him too." I nodded just as Mom ended the sports talk and steered the conversation toward Sally and James' relationship. Dion and I shared a conspiratorial smirk when the couple hogged most of the attention. That was until James brought up a desk clerk vacancy that had opened up at his office.

"I can arrange for either one of you to get started as soon as possible if you want. The pay is not half bad, not to mention the benefits, and you'll have ample opportunity to move up in the firm." His gaze flickered between Dion and me. I stuffed food into my mouth and chewed slowly to avoid answering and ignored the eerily similar flashes of annoyances in my father's and Jamie's eyes.

"I have a job I love, so no, thank you," Dion answered flippantly, his smile a little too tight at the edges.

"Oh, for goodness's sake!" Dad tossed his napkin on the table. "Skipping from one bar to the next, playing for a dead crowd of thirty people is not a job! It's high time you both got your heads out of the clouds and started behaving like responsible adults. You're not a rock star, Dion, and you..." Dad let out a weary sigh, shaking his head. "I don't even know if you have ambitions, Dianna. As far-fetched as Dion's dreams are, at least he has a goal in mind. What is your endgame, dear?"

"My dreams are not as far-fetched as you might think. We've actually been invited to go on a countrywide tour as the opening act for The Jaywalkers," Dion cut in before I could answer our father. I wasn't sure if he did that for my benefit or out of indignation from Dad once again trivializing what he did.

"I may not have any grand aspirations or anything, Dad, but that doesn't mean I'll chain myself to a dead-end job just for the sake of it. I have two jobs that I love and am fine where I am for the moment," I answered in a measured tone, pushing my food away. The little I had already eaten settled like sour milk in my gut and the taste had turned rancid in my mouth. Okay, maybe I was exaggerating about loving my jobs, but I wasn't unhappy with them. And I was sure I was at least happier where I was than in some stuffy office with my dad and brother looking over my shoulder all the time.

"Oh, please! A Flowers working as a shopkeeper and teaching children how to scribble on paper with crayons. What was the point of shelling out all that money for college, then? I thought that since you went against my wishes and enrolled for a degree in fine arts, you would at least make use of your talent. Work in a gallery or sell your paintings… something. Instead, you're—"

"Daniel!" My mother called out in a sharp tone, cutting him off mid-tirade. "Not here. You're being loud and people are watching."

Of course she didn't stop him to defend me, but because people were watching. They were always watching, and as the oh-so-perfect Flowers family, we couldn't have them see us stumble or mess up. We were Flowers and Grangers. My father was the director of the hospital and a respected surgeon. My mother was involved in most, if not all, of the town's fundraising and charity committees. Uncle Hank was the mayor, grandfather was the priest, golden boy Jamie was the lawyer, Mirabelle was getting her PhD, and Juno was the star athlete at Mystic Cove High.

Even Dion was making something of himself with his

band, even if Dad didn't want to admit it, but I was…still not the daughter my dad wanted. You'd think with two other daughters to pick up the slack, he'd let me off the hook…at least a little.

CHAPTER 2

*B*runch ended on a sour note. I watched Mom, Dad, and Juno drive back home. Jamie and Sally were already gone, and I declined a ride back home from Dion.

"Don't let your dad get to you, sweetheart. He just wants what's best for you and just happens to be going about things the wrong way," Granddad said, trying to comfort me as we stared out at the sea in front of The Black Pearl. The water was still, the waves rolling lazily onto the shore, and not a boat or surfer to be seen. The beach was not as packed as it usually was; maybe everyone was having a lazy Sunday in. He was waiting for Uncle Hank to finish up his conversation with a local Mystic Cove businessman and drive him home.

"Don't think I don't know you'd whoop for joy if I told you I quit my job at The Book Coven, Grandpa," I teased, bumping my hip against his and eliciting a gruff chuckle from him.

"That transparent, am I?" he asked with a wry grin, his eyes tracking the erratic path of a seagull overhead.

"You're not exactly known for keeping a cool head where

Beverley Barnes is concerned. What's the deal between the two of you anyway?" I asked even though I knew he wouldn't tell me why he and my boss hated each other with the passion of a thousand suns.

It was so bad that my grandfather ordered books and stationery online instead of stepping foot into The Book Coven. Whenever Beverley wanted to donate to the church, she did it under one of her daughters' names. But there were times when it was unavoidable, such as when Beverly volunteered for charity events hosted by her coven, and the two of them always made sure to give the other a wide berth lest they spark World War III.

As a young girl, I had assumed that my grandfather had something against the witch community in general, but no. His congregation had a healthy number of witches and warlocks, three vampires, a whole lot of humans, and shifters. It was just Beverley Barnes he had a problem with.

"It's nothing, big baby girl— Greta, hey! Is it time for your shift already?" I was taken aback by the sudden change of topic before I realized he was talking to the pretty brunette wearing the white and blue uniform of The Black Pearl.

"Hi, Father Granger. Yeah, I just had to make a short stop at the commune to change into my uniform. That was a great service today, by the way. Are we still on for choir practice tomorrow?" she asked, casting a shy glance and smile my way.

Vampire, my senses screamed at me. I didn't know what it was about her that made me think she was, but I had the uncanny ability to sus out supers from a crowd of humans. And the pallor of her complexion and the fact that every inch of her skin, except her hands, was covered confirmed my suspicions.

Although the sun was out in its full glory, the heat of

summer was past us, so I could forgive her for dressing so stuffily, but it was muggy as heck. No one would willingly dress like that in this weather except tightwads like James, whom I was pretty sure slept in his bespoke suits, and vampires.

"Six p.m. on the dot. Have you met my granddaughter Dianna? She has the voice of an angel and used to be the star of our choir until she decided that the Christian faith is a hoax." Granddad laughed, throwing an arm around my shoulders and squeezing me to his side. I resisted the urge to roll my eyes at his quip. The only reason any of my siblings and I went to church or joined the choir was because our parents forced us to attend. The second we stopped living under their roof, the number of times we'd been inside the house of the Lord had dwindled. Juno was unfortunate enough to be the only child still under Mom and Dad's care, so if she wanted to keep any of her privileges, they said jump and she asked how high.

"I don't believe I have, but I think I've seen her at the bookstore. I've been meaning to come inside for a while now, but I'm always in a hurry, taking care of one errand or another. I'm Greta Jennings." She held out her hand for a shake. It was cool to the touch, much like the vampires I'd dealt with before.

"Dianna. Are you new in town?" I asked her.

"Mmm-hmm. Moved in about a month ago after Father Granger found me struggling to cope with my...condition." She gave me a flash of her baby canines. "If it weren't for him, I would have been an unemployed, unhinged vampire caught in the grip of bloodlust. I should get inside before the manager rips me a new one. It was nice meeting you, Dianna. Have a nice day, Father."

"Picked up another stray, Grandad?" I asked quietly, watching Greta disappear through the doors to the restaurant. Aside from leading the church, he ran a commune for runaways, troubled teens—and in rare cases, people like Greta who found themselves suddenly thrust into this paranormal world of ours. People who, for whatever reason, had been turned into vampires or whatever else against their will and had no idea how to handle this sudden change. He set them up with a room in the commune, helped them get a job somewhere in town, and was their guiding hand until they got back on their feet again.

"You know I don't like that word, Dianna. Greta is a nice girl but very timid. I don't know how much of that has to do with what happened to her before I found her or if it was just her personality before the change."

I let out a pained groan before he completed what he wanted to say. My grandfather was as transparent as the lenses of his glasses.

"And let me guess, you want me to be her friend? Introduce her to a few people? You've seen the crowd I hang out with, Gramps. If Greta is as shy as you say she is, she's going to run screaming for the hills after one hangout with the crew."

The old man had the audacity to scoff at my claim. "Oh, please! The lot of you may walk around dressed like Marilyn Manson groupies, but I've seen firsthand what big softies you are under all that leather and chains. Incidentally, Greta is eager to move out of the commune and happens to be looking for an apartment at the moment. But she can't afford to pay the rent on her own." He let out a mock gasp. "Why, Dianna, didn't I hear you tell your parents that you were planning on moving out of your dingy apartment as soon as you saved up enough money to move into a decent place? I believe a solution just fell into your lap."

"You're an incorrigible old man." I laughed and kissed him on the forehead.

~*~

The work week dawned way too early for my tastes. Beverley was already behind the counter when I walked into the store with our coffee orders from Jumpin' Beans next door.

"Morning, dear," she chirped brightly, fussing over a fresh arrangement of begonias on the counter. Every few days, there were new flower arrangements placed strategically in the store. She already had the incense burning and a Lo-Fi mediation playlist playing.

"Morning, Bev. Beautiful flowers as always." I complimented the arrangement and set her venti almond milk latte in front of her. She took a swig of the drink and moaned in pleasure before gesturing for the paper bag in my other hand for her bagel sandwich.

"This is the food of the goddesses," she moaned after taking a huge bite and glancing at the clock mounted on the wall behind her. "We've got forty-five minutes before the shop opens for business. Why don't we head on to the back?"

A thrill of exhilaration zapped through me. My smile went all the way to my ears and threatened to split my face in two. "Another lesson?" I all but jogged to the storeroom-slash-whatever room Beverly required it to be. She dipped her head in a nod and gestured for me to precede her through the doors.

One of the reasons I loved working at The Book Coven so much was because of all the witchcraft lessons Beverley gave me on the side. As a human, I did not possess the innate ability to manipulate mana like all naturally born witches and warlocks. I couldn't conjure up fantastical objects with a simple snap of my fingers. But there were potions and spells I could do that did not require a person to have magic.

The storeroom was stacked with stock that was yet to be unpacked, special book orders waiting to be picked up, a couple of gardening tools, miscellaneous items like Christmas and Halloween decorations, and some old paintings that used to adorn the walls.

"Are we still doing healing tonics?" I asked, hooking my bag and spider web-patterned, crocheted cardigan on the coat rack.

"What else would we be doing?" Beverley took a sip of her latte and walked to one of the cabinets in the storeroom and started picking out jars of herbs.

"I was thinking we could move beyond that. Maybe you could teach me something more exciting like... I don't know... A hex to make all of my enemies' teeth fall out or something?"

Beverley arched a brow at my suggestion, her lips pursed in bemusement with thin lines flaring out from the corners of her mouth. "I am not teaching you these skills so that you can go around placing hexes and curses on people who cause you the slightest inconvenience. If that's what you've been after this whole time, then we can call it quits right here and now." She splayed her fingers on the only wide table in the room and speared me with a challenging glare.

A cold shiver skittered up my spine as the air around us grew heavy and a metallic taste bloomed on my tongue. I wanted to ask Beverley if she was using magic on me but found I couldn't speak, so I shook my head instead.

The suffocating atmosphere disappeared and with it, the pressure on my chest. I sucked in a deep breath of fresh air. "I didn't mean to come off as if I had an ulterior motive or to sound ungrateful, Bev. It's just that we've been doing nothing but making healing tonics and tisanes. I wanted us to move on to something a little more..." I waved a hand in the air, searching for the perfect word.

"Something a little flashier? Dangerous? Daring?" Beverley filled in the blanks.

"Yeah, all of that," I replied with an awkward shrug.

Beverley shook her head in a distinctly maternal manner and came to stand beside me, pulling me into a vanilla-scented hug. "Patience, my dear. Everything must be done in its proper order. All great witches and warlocks are great because they have a strong and stable foundation. The things you want to learn have the potential to cause harm to others if done carelessly. So, before I equip you with those skills, I need to teach you how to heal first…just in case." She gave me a gentle squeeze, and I nodded in understanding.

In the remaining time until the store opened, I diligently followed Beverley's instructions as she talked me through instructions for herbal concoctions to boost fertility.

The day ticked by at a snail's pace. I mean, working at a bookstore is not exactly an adrenaline rush, but today was especially dull. Aside from my morning potion lessons, that is. By the time the clock struck four, I was counting down the minutes until five-thirty when I could get out of there. And yet, there was a part of me that dreaded going back to my apartment and the stifling loneliness that waited for me. Since there was a lull in the shop, I stepped out to the store-room and sent a text on my friend group chat asking if anyone was up for a round or two of drinks at the bar or maybe catching a movie, but everyone was busy doing their own thing for the day.

When I stepped back into the store, the peaceful atmosphere I'd left earlier was nowhere to be felt. Beverley was going off at two shamefaced boys around my age, waving her hands wildly in the air. They couldn't rush out of the store fast enough when she was done with them.

"Urgh!" Beverley growled in frustration, shaking a fist in the air and glaring at the boys' retreating backs. "If it weren't against Coven Law, I would have transfigured their sniveling butts into the rats they are."

"You okay there, Bev? I think you got smoke coming out of your ears. What did they do?" I flicked my head in the direction of the exit. My boss let out another deranged growl before taking in deep, calming breaths and straightening out the bell sleeves of her blouse and tightening the knot of her sixties-inspired hair bandana.

"They were being horrible human beings is what happened. What is it about people that they have to lash out in horrible ways just because something or someone is different from what they're used to? I can tolerate ignorance from young children and maybe newcomers to Mystic Cove, but when you've lived here all your life and insist on perpetuating harmful stereotypes and fanning the flames of hatred and ignorance, I just want to—" She let out a frustrated scream and literally spat fire like a bloody dragon, scorching the counter.

"Jeez!" I yelped, stepping back before she turned her aggression on me. Wide-eyed, feeling equal parts fear and wonder, I stared agog as Beverley burped and a ring of smoke floated out of her mouth.

"Apologies, dear." She waved the smoke away. "It's just that those boys were harassing Parker and saying the nastiest things to the poor boy. It made my blood boil."

"Parker?" I ran the name through my memories and came up blank. I didn't know anyone named Parker. "I'm not following. Who are we talking about?"

Beverley waved a hand over the scorch marks on the counter, and they sort of seeped into the wood and were replaced by the original shine and polish of the redwood countertop. "Parker Smith, the young man who works at the funeral home. He's painfully shy and sweet as a sugarplum. He was in here to pick up his monthly reads and those… those litter terrors started spewing filth at him simply because he is a zombie. Honestly, the mistreatment that boy receives at the hands of the townsfolk makes me ashamed to call myself a Mystic Cove local." She tsked her tongue.

My mouth made an O shape when I realized who she was talking about. I'd never met him before, but I still remembered the uproar that Parker Smith caused when he moved to town two years ago.

As far as everyone knew, zombies were walking dead creatures who feasted off human brains and flesh. People had been up in arms when they discovered what he was, demanding he be forced out of Mystic Cove. Weirdly enough, it was one of the few times my grandfather and Beverley put aside their differences to advocate for Parker's right to settle down here.

Unlike what pop culture would have you believe, zombies look nothing like the creatures from *The Walking Dead* or *Train to Busan*. They were somewhere between humans and vampires—not dead, but not really living either. They were extremely rare and small in number, according to Beverley and her coven. Zombies lived in close-knit clans and mostly kept to themselves. Information on their race was scarce.

"Is he gone already?" I craned my neck as if I would spot him lurking behind the shelves or something. I couldn't count the number of times I kept saying that I would introduce myself, but it kept falling to the wayside. When he first moved here, I did some deep dive research on zombies, but like I said, information on them was scarce. Most of what I found on the net was all that brain-eating nonsense. The only relevant information I had was what I got from older witches like Beverley and an anonymous netizen from a forum online. My mystery friend lived in a town much like Mystic Cove and knew of a small clan of zombies living in her town too. Like me, she was fascinated with the supernatural and the occult, so she told me everything she knew about zombies—including the fact that they ate regular human food and not humans themselves.

"Unfortunately. He didn't even wait long enough to pick up his books. He fled out of here like a wounded puppy. Those bloody brats," she murmured the last part under her breath. We ended up closing the shop half an hour early since no one else came into the store, and I decided to go watch a movie by myself.

A small voice nagged at the back of my brain that I could have just visited my family if I was that hard-up for company, but as much as I loved them—frustrating as they were—I valued my peace of mind even more. As long as Dad and I weren't on the same page, I preferred him in small doses.

Coincidentally, the movie theater was having a *Resident Evil* marathon. Since I had zombies on the brain, I figured it was a better choice than the other marathon they were having in the second theater room—*The Fast and Furious.* Pure cringe.

I inhaled a hotdog before stepping into the cinema with my order of jellybeans and a jumbo-sized cola.

There were four other people in the theater when I walked in. A couple was seated on the second row at the front, and they were already necking without a care in the world like they were sitting on their living room couch. I shared a sneer with the older gentleman who was seated in the row behind them. I walked to the very last row of seats, where another man was sitting at the opposite end from where I was. I almost tripped over my feet when I got a look at how painfully beautiful he was.

Shaggy white hair fell over his eyes and thick-rimmed glasses. I got a side profile view of his perfectly sculpted face; his jawline could cut glass, as my mother would say. I placed my bag in the seat next to me and settled down without looking away from him. Rude, I know, but I was trying to get him to look my way so that I could get a better look at all that beauty.

Instead, his posture grew tense as he slumped down in his seat, pushed his glasses up the bridge of his upturned nose, and dug his phone out of his pocket, which he studied studiously.

Ten minutes into the movie, I was barely paying attention to what was happening on the screen. "Jellybeans?" I asked him, when I realized that he had a jumbo-sized smoothie and nothing else.

"I'm fine, thank you." His voice was a quiet whisper, and he only glanced my way briefly before turning his attention back to the screen. The way his shoulders were hunched was a clear sign that he didn't want to have any interaction with me, so I told myself that I would try again between movies. The chance never came. He shot out of his seat the second the end credits started. I left halfway into the second movie when I couldn't stand watching the couple up front going at it anymore and being all lovey-dovey.

Two days later, I was starting to think the world had it in for me and couldn't resist rubbing happy couples in my face. I found out that two of my friends had hooked up, and the reason we barely hung out together anymore was because they were spending all their free time together. I could barely sleep a wink at night, and not just because of the rats. My cheap apartment had paper-thin walls, and it was painfully obvious the man in the apartment next to mine had found a new boyfriend.

And then there was my freaking brother and his new girlfriend. We'd only met Sally a couple of days ago, but just the night before, he sent the family group chat into a tizzy when he "accidentally" sent pictures of a selection of engagement rings. My mother hadn't shut up about it since.

"We're nowhere near Valentine's Day, so why the sudden infestation of couples?" I huffed, glaring at the couple who had just left the bookstore after making a purchase. I did not realize that I'd asked the question out loud until Beverley looked up from her laptop. She was seated on one of the couches, going over the Book Coven's finances and having tea.

"What was that, dear?" She took her spectacles off and placed them on the armrest of the couch and picked up her teacup. I glanced around the shop and saw that all the other customers were still having a look around, so I walked around the counter to take a seat next to my boss. I grabbed a chewy, chocolate chip, ginger cookie and demolished it in two bites, chewing angrily.

"Someone's hangry," Beverley teased when I went for another cookie. She took the liberty of reaching for the pot of tea and pouring some for me.

"More like lonely. Do you know how long it's been since I've been on a date?" I ranted.

"I'm afraid I don't, Dianna dear." Beverley smiled, her eyes alight with amusement.

"Too dang long!" I complained, slumping down in the seat and sulking like a child.

"Whatever happened to what's-his-face, the singer you dated before? I thought things were getting serious between you two."

"You mean Lucas?" I rolled my eyes at the mere mention of his name. "We broke up ages ago. He was pretty to look at but as interesting as a wet carrot. And he was kinda creeping me out with all the songs he wrote about me. One or two songs I was cool with, but a whole sappy album?" I shook my head, fighting off a shudder. Lucas had been turning into a level ten clinger, and I wanted no part in that.

"Funny, I believe you've used that excuse before. Are the

men of Mystic Cove really that boring, or do you have a short attention span?" Beverley asked, turning her perceptive gaze on me. With that single look, I felt like she'd flipped back the curtain on my innermost thoughts and laid my soul bare.

"Maybe I have high standards," I shot back, reaching for my third cookie. Beverley shook her head and started to say something but then the door to the store opened and her granddaughter Sophia and Sophia's husband, Jacob, walked in.

I went to assist a customer who wanted to pay while the three of them caught up. Sophia was all smiles and glowing like a polished gem under her husband's besotted gaze. She reminded me of Olivia, who owned Jumpin' Beans next door, and her boyfriend, Adrian. They all had that same gooey love-struck look about them, and it was all thanks to my boss.

"Hold the phone…" I whispered at the brilliant flash of an idea that struck me. I wouldn't have this short attention span problem if I were with the man I was meant to be with for the rest of my life, would I?

"How come you've never offered to set me up?" I asked Beverly after Sophia and Jacob left.

"What?" Beverley frowned in confusion, clearing up the empty cookie tray and tea set.

"You've set up all these couples around town, and they're all going strong. Why don't you find my match so I can just skip over all the boring stuff and get right to my happily ever after?"

Beverley let out a dry chuckle. "It's not like I click my finger and the perfect man shows himself to me, Dianna. It's not an exact science, and I've yet to meet a man I felt would be compatible with you—"

"So you're saying I'm undateable, is that it?" I cut in.

Beverley's eyes went wide. "What? That's not what I'm saying. Are you sure this is what you really want? Or are you challenging me to find your match just because you're lazy?"

"I don't know. A little bit of both? What does it matter, though? If you find my soulmate, I'm guaranteed to never get bored of him and we can ride off into the sunset or whatever," I answered with a flippant wave of the hand.

The corners of Beverley's mouth tipped down in an unimpressed frown. "That's not how love or relationships work, Dianna. Two people can be fated for each other in every way, but if they don't put any effort into making the relationship work, it can still turn sour. I've known mates who have driven each other to madness and made themselves miserable or treated their significant others horribly, all because they think that just because someone is their mate, they cannot find love elsewhere. So, I will ask again— are you sure this is this what you really want?"

I wasn't sure, but I said yes anyway.

CHAPTER 3

PARKER

"There you go, Maggie. Pretty as a picture and ready for your family's last goodbyes." I smiled down at the girl who looked like she was only taking a nap and could wake up any moment. Except she was too still to be sleeping and the flush of life was missing from her cheeks, replaced by the light strokes of blush I'd just applied to lessen the pallor of death that clung to her.

I'd dressed Maggie in a sunflower patterned dress her mother had delivered to the funeral home yesterday morning, along with the chocolate brown wig she'd asked me to use. It didn't match the original color of Maggie's natural hair, but apparently Maggie had favored it over the other wigs her parents bought her. Only fifteen, Maggie should have been having the time of her life with the rest of her cheerleading friends, doing dumb stuff and living it up in her teenage years. But she'd been diagnosed with leukemia a year prior, and despite the aggressive treatments she received, her immune system was too compromised to fight off a pneumonia infection. And that's how she ended up on my table.

"What do you think, Mags? Did I do a great job, or did I make you look like a clown?" I asked out loud, even though I was the only person in the room. At my question, a slight breeze tickled the nape of my neck and caressed my face almost playfully. My lips curled in a small smile to match. "I'll take that to mean that you like it then." I brushed the wisps of her bangs away from her eyes and started to pack away the makeup kit when I heard footsteps come down the stairs to the mortuary.

"Parker?" Mrs. Graham's voice called out. A second later, she appeared at the doorway, her brows knitted in a frown and eyes scanning the wide room before settling on me. "Were you talking to someone? I thought I heard voices."

My face went hot. If I still had the ability to blush, I would have been as red as a chili pepper. "Oh, no. I was just talking to…uh…" I waved my hand awkwardly across Maggie's body on the table. Mrs. Graham arched her eyebrows, the expression she wore unreadable. "I sometimes talk to my clients since I'm the only one down here most days. It makes the work…less morbid, I guess." I adjusted my glasses and ran a hand through my hair only to have the shaggy strands flop back over my eyes.

"I see," Mrs. Graham said, but her tone and the look in her eyes said otherwise. Clearing her throat, she stepped deeper into the room and came to stand at the head of the table where Maggie lay. Her brown eyes flashed with sympathy as she stared down at the girl. "It's always more difficult when they're still children; she barely got to experience life. The wake will be starting soon, so we need to transport her body. But before that, I wanted to have a talk with you."

I hated it when people said that. *We need to talk.* Such innocuous words on their own, but strung together, they were often a harbinger of doom. Every time a conversation was preceded by those words, I just knew that my life was about to be turned on its head. Given my precarious standing in this town, a series of scenarios ran through my mind, ranging from Mrs. Graham finally caving in to the pressure to fire me, to her telling me there was an angry mob outside to run me out of town with torches and pitchforks in hand. In a town run amok by witches, vampires, and werewolves, I found it weird that zombies were where the humans chose to draw the line.

If I had a nickel for every time someone accused me of feasting on the bodies that passed through the funeral home or—*gag*—molesting the cadavers, I'd be able to afford a better trailer home. Mrs. Graham was a great boss and had gone to great lengths to defend me against such horrible rumors, but there was only so much she could take. Especially when there was a very vocal group in the community threatening to use the services of a funeral home one town over instead of this one.

"Is something wrong? Another complaint?" I took my latex gloves off and chucked them into the trash can, then I took off the apron and hung it on the coat rack.

"No, no. It's not anything bad, so stop frowning so much. You'll get old before your time," she teased and walked over to my desk, pulling out a chair and sitting down. "You're aware that I have been talking about retiring for a while now," she began.

I nodded, clasping my hands behind my back and surreptitiously breathing in through my nose. "Did you find someone to take over for you already?" *And are they okay with me staying on as the mortician despite my condition?* I wasn't sure I wanted to hear the answer to that question, so I kept it to myself for the moment. Thankfully, my voice came out steady and strong, all my anxieties remaining hidden beneath the surface.

"Actually, I haven't found anyone yet. I was hoping you'd changed your mind and gave my offer some thought."

I balked, taking a step back as if to run away. Two weeks ago, Mrs. Graham and her husband offered me the position of funeral director. I wanted to accept it so bad. Being a mortician or funeral director was the complete opposite of what I wanted to be growing up. It was leagues away from the life I led before I became what I was now, but I had grown to love the job. And I'd grown to love this town, even if it didn't love me back. And that's exactly why I couldn't take the job.

"I already told you my reasons for declining. The people can barely tolerate me handling the bodies of their loved ones. If I became the funeral director—"

Mrs. Graham held her hand out and stopped me mid-sentence. "I can't and won't defend what some of the citizens of this town have put you through, Parker. That said, it is not you who should be hiding from the world or walking about hanging your head in shame when you have done nothing wrong. If they want to drive an hour to the next town for a funeral home, that's on them. It's certainly no skin off my nose. If you want this job, and I can tell that you do, then take it."

"Are you sure about this?" I tried again, wrapping one hand around the opposite wrist and squeezing it to the point that the tips of my fingers started to tingle from the lack of blood flow.

Mrs. Graham gave me a fond, albeit exasperated, smile. Slapping her hands on her thighs, she stood up. "No matter how many times you ask that question, my answer will remain the same. I can't think of a better person to hand the home over to than you, and I was hoping you'd say yes so that we could begin your training today."

My jaw dropped. "T-today? But that means—" I cut

myself off, my tongue dry and heavy from the implications of what my boss was saying. I would have to deal with the bereaved family members and take care of all the planning for Maggie's service.

I glanced at her lifeless body on the table as if she would give me an answer. And maybe she did. The chilly breeze from earlier was back and gave me a slight nudge toward the door. "Okay," I muttered to myself, and then repeated a little louder and more assertively. "I can do this. I'll do it. I'll start training for the job."

"Wonderful! But first, I'll need you to change into a suit or something more presentable." Mrs. Graham beamed up at me. Her request wasn't an issue since my home was a five-minute walk away. I had a trailer home situated in—believe it or not—the Mystic Cove graveyard, right across the road from the church. Morbid, I know. But it was the only place in town where my neighbors weren't terrified to death—pun intended—of my presence, and the rent was dirt cheap.

My living in a graveyard only further reinforced the town's prejudices against me, but there wasn't a landlord in town willing to let me sign a lease for an apartment. Not after the big stink that was kicked up in the last community I'd lived in.

~*~

My social battery was at an all-time low. I hated dealing with people— humans especially. But dealing with grieving and somewhat irrational parents was even more draining than I thought possible.

By the time I was headed home, I was ready to tumble head-first into my bed. But I had a standing date with my only friend in this town, Emil Deschamps, a vampire who was even more of a recluse than me. He lived in a sprawling house of log and glass at the base of the mountain, close to the skiing resort, but not so close that nosy tourists would inadvertently make their way onto his property.

I can't even tell you how the two of us became friends, only that he talked to me out of nowhere one day at Jumpin' Beans. I was engrossed in the paranormal thriller I was reading at the time and my third cup of vanilla iced coffee when this citrine-eyed dude sat at my table and asked me if the book was really *so* good that I could barely take my eyes off it for a second. Any sense of social mores fled in an instant and I'd gone off on a total fanboy spiel, not only telling Emil about the specific book I was reading at the time, but the absolute masterpiece-ness of the whole freaking series. The dude sat there, listening to me embarrass myself with a smug smirk on his face just to eventually introduce himself as Emil Deschamps—a.k.a., the author who wrote the very series I had been reading.

I wanted to crawl into a hole and die—again—every time I remembered our first encounter, but hey, I got to read his books for free before they were even published now, so I guess geeking out worked in my favor for once.

The parking space in front of the coffee shop was taken up, so I had to drive around the block until I found a free space to park my car and made the five-minute walk to Jumpin' Beans. I walked with my gaze fixed on the paved sidewalk, not wanting to meet anyone's gaze and to avoid the glaring light from the day's fading sunlight. Ever since I underwent the change and became a zombie, my eyesight was sharper than it used to be, but usually only in dark or dimly lit areas. Natural sunlight was especially harsh on my pale, almost white pupils, which was why I wore glasses with UV filtering lenses.

My phone buzzed with a text from Emil just as I was about to step into the coffee shop; he was running late. I hadn't brought anything to read or keep me busy while I waited for him other than my phone. The coffee shop was pretty packed for mid-day, and I did not relish hogging a table by myself while I waited. My gaze landed on the store next door, The Book Coven.

I hadn't been there since the incident last week when I let two young men push me to the verge of tears with a few words. Pathetic! But in my defense, I'd been having a rough day overall. Someone had broken into my trailer while I was at work and ransacked the place. Nothing was stolen, which almost made the whole thing worse. They didn't need any money or anything. They'd only wanted to terrorize me. I'd come home to find my living room and bedroom in a mess and someone had left what I'd been told by the police was a pig's brain on my pillows.

I had an inkling who'd done it. Some kids from MC High had been ditching their lessons to smoke pot and get drunk in the graveyard over the last couple of weeks, and I'd told them off for wandering too close to my home and littering the cemetery. I'd said as much to the officers who'd responded to my call, and they'd promised to get back to me after questioning the kids. I'd been pretty clear in my descriptions of them, but here we were. Almost a full week later and I hadn't heard a thing. C'est la vie, I guess. Needless to say, I'd been too embarrassed to go back to The Book Coven after running off with my tail between my legs.

Beverley Barnes was one of the sweetest women I knew, always ready with a smile, tea, and cookies whenever I stopped in, at least once a month, in search of new reading material. The fact that she'd seen me cower to a bunch of eighteen-year-olds was mortifying.

"Buck up, Parker," I could already hear her saying. "Since when do we let the bullies win?" Beverley would be too kind to judge me for my hasty retreat. Girding my loins, I walked over to the store and loosed a breath I wasn't aware I was holding when I realized that except for Beverley, there was hardly anyone else there. I thought I caught a flash of blonde hair disappearing behind the door that led to the back—the mysterious part-timer that was always conveniently "working in the back" whenever I came around. There was an older gentleman at the counter who paid for his purchases and nodded at me in acknowledgment before leaving.

"Parker, what a nice surprise! A lucky one too. We just got a new batch of books, including a sci-fi *Star Wars*-esque epic that I think you might like." Beverly waved me over, a wide smile across her face. Stepping away from the cash register, Beverley leaned on the counter, her friendly eyes assessing me and missing nothing. "You look dapper; is it a special day? Hot date, perhaps?" She gave me a saucy smirk.

And there came that sensation again, the one where it felt like I should be blushing, my cheeks red hot and the tips of my ears all pinked out. But I was an undead monster and incapable of any of that anymore. Frankly, I still wasn't sure about the mechanics of my body, and I'd been a zombie for nearly a decade.

I mean, I had the same organs as a normal human being, but for whatever reason, my heart pumped blue blood and my heart rate was a tenth of that of a healthy, normal human being. I bled blue, and everything worked just as it should—better even. Enhanced senses, enhanced strength, and enhanced healing capabilities, all of which was both a blessing and curse. And yet I didn't blush. And I didn't need to eat or sleep as regularly as humans did; although, I kept a daily routine to have a sense of normalcy in my life.

I had died—I remembered my death far too clearly—but then I woke up. And not like a near-death experience. I was full-on, been embalmed, had a funeral, and was about to be buried in the ground dead. I shuddered to think what would have happened if I'd woken up half an hour later, after the coffin had been sealed and dirt had been piled on top six-feet thick. Of course, waking up at your own funeral service is not something I'd recommend either. I didn't even know my so-called friends and family could run that fast.

Like vampires, I was one of the living dead. But unlike vampires, I didn't need human blood, or any human flesh, to survive. I ate food just like humans when I needed it, which wasn't often. But *how* I'd come back to life, or *why*, were questions I hadn't been able to answer. Was it magic? A curse? Would I die again? Did I really want to know?

"Nothing of the sort. You know as well as I do that the dating pool for zombies in this town is slim pickings. I doubt that even you, with your magic touch, could successfully set me up on a date," I said with a wry twist of my lips. I knew immediately that that had been the wrong thing to say when her eyes lit up.

"Is that a challenge I hear, young man?"

"W-what? Of course not, I was only saying— I didn't mean to imply that I wanted you to, you know…enspell a girl for me or anything. I'm wearing a suit because Mrs. Graham is training me to take over her duties once she retires," I sputtered, feeling flustered and too hot in my blazer.

"Oh, congratulations. I had no idea Susan was planning on retiring. But back to the topic at hand, I don't know what you think you know of my matchmaking, but I can assure you that I do not in any way use spells or love potions to coerce or induce feelings of infatuation or affection in the people I set up with each other. Any love that blossoms between my couples is freely given," she explained, her countenance unexpectedly solemn.

"I didn't think that you did anything of the sort. I apologize if I offended you by implying anything like that." I scratched my eyebrow and checked the time on the clock mounted on the wall behind her. This conversation had taken an unexpected turn and was taking up more time than I'd meant.

"None taken, sweetheart. I just wanted to know that anyone I set you up with would meet up with you of their own free will. Well, to an extent, as I usually operate by setting up blind dates. But any romance that arises from the date has nothing to do with me and everything to do with you and your partner."

"You sound like you already have someone in mind," I said cautiously, quelling the rising excitement bubbling in my gut. I didn't want to raise my hopes, soaring high past the clouds only for them to splat like a half-cooked pancake on the hard ground.

Beverly pursed her lips. She briefly glanced at the door that led to the storeroom and then up to the ceiling. I could almost see the gears tuning in her head. She started to shake her head and paused, drumming her fingers on the countertop.

"Beverley?" I prodded when she just kept frowning as if she was trying to figure out a tricky puzzle.

"I think I might have someone in mind. Do you want me to set the two of you up?"

Did I? I blinked at her like an idiot, a riot of emotions stirring within me. I'd heard about Beverley's matchmaking before. I'd even seen the results, and at one point I'd been so lonely that I considered going to her for help. But I was so shy and awkward that I never gathered the courage to say anything. And then Emil and I became friends and the fangs of isolation, desperation, and sadness weren't sunk so deep into my jugular anymore. I could breathe a little easier. But there was a part of me that wondered if I would end up alone for as long as I lived without anyone to call my own. A lover, a family, or a clan of my own.

I used to have one—a family and a clan. But they both had abandoned me when I needed them the most. I'd watched helplessly as the bonds I thought would hold strong, come what may, crumbled like a house of cards at the mere whisper of a storm to come. Did I want to set myself up for another heartbreak like that again?

If it ain't broke, don't fix it, right? I was content with my life as it was right then. I kept my head down and did my job. I had a friend. I was fine. *I am fine.*

Are you, though? a voice whispered at the back of my mind. Was I really fine, meandering from one day to another, my mental state only held together by a shoestring? Was I fine with Emil as my only friend and confidant? I mean, I had Mrs. Graham, Beverley, and Father Granger, who helped me a ton when I first moved here, but we weren't that close.

"Don't you think you should warn the poor woman first? In this case, I think you should suspend your blind date rule and tell her who you're setting her up with," I replied. Coming from me, that was a resounding *yes*, and Beverley knew it. She rolled her eyes at my comment.

"Never you fear. The girl I have in mind will be beside herself with joy once she realizes who her date is. Give me a few days to set everything up."

~*~

I'd forgotten to buy my books. Again. I left The Book Coven in a daze and ran into Emil right outside Jumpin' Beans' front door. He ushered me to our usual booth and told me about a trio of tourists who'd gotten lost and wound up on his property and how he scared the living daylights out of them, but I was barely keeping up with what he was saying. In my head, I was building up this image of my mystery woman. What she looked like, her hobbies, the sound of her voice and laughter. I had a feeling she would either be a witch or a vampire; they were pretty accepting of zombies. More so than humans, at least. Especially the vampires, since both of our species were technically "undead."

Shifters… I couldn't picture myself on a date with any of the wolves from Mystic Cove. They were scary and… I'm not sure how to describe it. Shifters were too "alive" for my taste. Filled with so much vitality, creatures of light, attuned to nature, while I was… Well, I was a creature of the dark. I defied the law of nature, the cycle of life and death. I had no definitive proof, but I didn't think I would do well with a shifter partner. And a human was so out of the question, it wasn't funny.

"What's wrong with you? You've been out of it since we got here. If I didn't know any better, I'd think you were high as a kite right now." Citrine, cat-like eyes peered at me. And I meant that literally. Something happened when Emil was changed into a vampire, morphing his pupils into thin slits like a cat or snake. I personally hated snakes, so I chose to describe them as cat-like.

"Nothing. Today was a long day is all." I shook my head. I didn't want to say anything about my date to Emil in case it bombed. "You were saying something about nosy tourists?"

He narrowed his eyes at me in suspicion. "I can smell lies, you know. But I'll let it slip this one time. And I finished talking about that minutes ago. I wanted to get your opinion on these cover art designs. I can't decide on one to use for my next book." He tapped the tablet he'd slipped in front of me. I hadn't even noticed it until now.

"Oh, wow! These are great!" I gushed, scrolling through the five variations of the gothic thriller book Emil had finished writing and was currently editing. "You got a new artist?" There was a noticeable difference in the style and color palettes of the designs from Emil's previous books.

"After that whole plagiarism fiasco? There was no way I would keep using the same artist again. The best part is that Dianna is a local artist. Communication is way faster and easier, and her rates are affordable because she hasn't blown up yet, but her socials are growing fast, so I might as well cash in before she becomes too sought after for me to nab."

"Dianna?" I queried. The name didn't ring a bell.

"Yeah. She calls herself Huntress online. Remember that epic *Castlevania* fan art I showed you?" Emil dragged his iPad over to his side and logged into his Instagram account and showed me a profile of a digital artist with almost two hundred and fifty thousand followers. Her profile was filled with original artwork and shots of her commissions and fan art from popular shows, games, and anime. It was mostly digital art, but there were a handful of paintings and lots of pencil and ink sketches as well.

"She's good," I commented, scrolling through her profile, pausing to admire the ones that I liked the most. I took a peek at her profile picture and it was a fierce drawing she'd done of the goddess Artemis wearing a crown of amaranth flowers.

"Right? I bet you she would jump at the chance to design characters for your game when you finally get your butt out of your head and go back to doing what you actually love instead of that depressing job of yours." Emil scowled at me.

I choked on my drink, some of it spewing out of my nose and spraying everywhere. Some of the drink went down the wrong pipe, turning me into a coughing, laughing, and crying mess.

"It's 'taking your head out of your butt!' How are you an author but keep butchering the most basic phrases?" I choked out, wiping the drink dribbling down my chin with a napkin.

"Humph," Emil said, taking his iPad back and wiping it down dramatically. "Well, 20,000 pre-orders say I'm a perfectly fine wordsmith."

"Only thanks to your editor," I quipped back. "I hope you pay her good."

"I know what she's worth," he replied, waving over Wendy, the waitress, to refill our drinks. Once she was gone, he went on, "So, I know I said I was going to let it slip, but I've changed my mind. What's really going on with you?"

CHAPTER 4

"Di! Di! Look it! I painted it good, right?" One of my students, six-year-old Beth Bennet, crashed into my shin and almost head-butted me in her rush to show me her completed landscape painting of the park where we were holding class. It was a miracle she didn't mess the whole thing up by smearing the still wet painting all over my jeans and holey T-shirt—courtesy of my unwanted rat guests, of course.

"Easy, Beebee. What did we say about running in art class?" I eased the little girl off me and gave one of her pigtails a playful little tug.

She gave me a gap-toothed grin, eyes sparkling with mischief. "But I'm not holding scissors or a pencil or paint-brush. See?" She spread her hands open, forgetting that she was holding her painting.

"Oops!" I grabbed the canvas before it dropped to the ground. "This is really good, Beebee. I reckon we can submit this as one of the pieces to be auctioned off to raise money for the children's home," I said, and I meant it. Of all my students, she showed the most potential to develop a real talent for painting, standing head and shoulders above her classmates. She had an eye for detail and using color that her friends didn't, and even though her paintings were what you'd expect from a child of her age, there was something more to them.

"Really?" She jumped up and down, clapping her hands like a seal.

I winced at the sound of her shrill giggles. "Not so loud, Beth!" I tapped my lips with my index finger, indicating that she should turn it down a notch. Her classmates looked up from their own canvases in curiosity, and a couple of parents who were there with their kids, not as part of our art program, scowled in our direction when Beth's squeals of laughter scared away the ducklings they were trying to feed.

"Sorry," Beth apologized sheepishly and then went on to ask me a ton of questions about the gallery. For a little kid, she was turning out to be quite the money shark, wanting to know how much of a cut she was going to get from the auction. Taking her hand, I led her back to our group and set up another canvas for her to paint on. Keeping her focused on painting was usually the only way to quiet her down.

There were eleven students in my class. After being stuck in a classroom all week, they'd all begged me to host the class outdoors. So I'd packed them and some art supplies into the gallery's minivan and drove us to the park. I'd brought my own sketch pad and started working on preliminary sketches of an art commission for an indie author's fantasy novel. This was the second author, after Emil Deschamps, to seek me out for a book cover design. Not gonna lie, my head had inflated to twice its size. I was starting to believe I could make an actual solid career out of this. If I had a steady stream of commissions coming in, then my father would stop hounding me about the lack of a solid stream of income. Additionally, Landon Grayson had approached me about showcasing some of my paintings and sketches in the gallery. He'd been on my case for the last year or so after I started teaching art classes at his school, but I'd always declined. You know how it is with artists and their work—no matter how many people tell you that what you do is phenomenally amazing, in your eyes, your work is always ugly as sin. In your mind, you are complete trash compared to other people and there's no way anyone would want to buy your stuff because why would they waste thousands on utter garbage?

But my confidence was starting to build now. I'd even submitted some of my old art pieces for the children's home fundraiser.

At eleven-thirty, I called the class to an end, half an hour earlier than we usually end the lesson so that I could drive everybody back in time for their parents to pick them up. And then I spent another hour making sure everything was packed up and chatting with the gallery employees. This was a time-wasting ploy until I could hop on my scooter and head over to Beverley's cottage for more lessons. After griping and moaning all week about the rats in my apartment, she'd snapped and told me she'd teach me to make charms and smudging that would keep the critters away from my stuff.

Before that, I stopped at a store owned by a warlock that sold magical items and everything needed to practice witchcraft. My house was filled with knick-knacks, charms, and an extensive collection of other witches' and warlocks' grimoires and books of shadows. The most interesting read I ever bought was a journal from a servant who claimed to have worked in the infamous Bluebeard's household back in the 1600s. It was quite the salacious read.

"Are these for real?" I asked Oliver, the store owner, pointing at a new collection of vampire skulls packed on the shelf closest to the cash register. Like me, Oliver was into the whole occult scene and dressed like a Victorian vampire. Half of his head was shaved, the rest of his hair dyed bright red and hanging down to his waist. His lips and nails were painted black, his eyes were rimmed with kohl, and his tattoos peeked out from the collar of his red silk shirt.

"Nah. Grayson and his cabal would have my head if I sold actual vampire skulls. Those are just Halloween decorations for the normies." He leaned forward and lowered his voice conspiratorially. "But if you want an actual vamp skull, I could hook you up. It would cost you a ton of money, though." As he spoke, I caught peeks of his modified forked tongue.

"That's too morbid, even for me." I shuddered. I didn't want to offend any of my vampire friends if they ever dropped by my place and found the skull of one of their own on my bookshelf. Besides, what would I do with a vampire skull, drink wine out of it? Moving on from the fake skulls, I checked out what else was new in the store, scoffing as I walked past the love charms section and checked out the jewelry.

You'd think I was a witch myself with all the clutter taking up space in my apartment. I really did need to move out ASAP. My phone rang as I was sifting through an array of voodoo dolls, wondering if it was a good idea to get one.

"Yello," I answered without checking the caller I.D.

"Dianna? It's Greta, Greta Jennings. Your grandfather gave me your phone number." It took me a minute to remember who she was, and then the image of the fresh-faced vampire from The Black Pearl came to mind.

"Oh, yeah. Hi, Greta, what can I do you for?" I placed a straw voodoo doll back on the shelf and went to pay for the mood ring and the dangling triple chain barbell I picked out for my industrial piercing.

"Father Granger mentioned that you were looking to move into a new apartment and that you may be on the lookout for a roommate. Since we're in the same boat, he suggested I give you a call," Greta began.

I paused in the action of digging my wallet out of my backpack and cast a narrow-eyed glare at the ceiling. Nosy old man! I let out an awkward, airy chuckle, tucking my phone between my ear and shoulder while I paid for my goods. "Listen, Greta, I don't know what my granddad told you, but I haven't found an apartment yet, and I still have like three months left on my lease."

"Oh." She sounded despondent. "Thing is, I already found an apartment that I like, and I was hoping to bring you on board—after you've seen it, of course. But if it's going to be a hassle to break your lease..." She let her sentence die off, and I let the silence hang for a minute as I gave it a thought. If I moved out early, I would lose my deposit. But considering how much money I'd had to spend on new clothes and replacing the food the rats had eaten...

"It might not be too much of a hassle," I finally said. "Where is this apartment and how much is the rent?"

Greta gave me all the details I needed and we agreed upon a time to check the apartment out on Monday during my lunch hour.

~*~

The smells wafting out of Beverley's home had my mouth watering the moment I stepped through her front door. Garlic, lemon, and ginger were the dominating aromas amongst the myriad of herbs and spices. The warm and yeasty scent of freshly baked bread had my stomach growling; I hadn't had anything to eat besides a banana for breakfast that morning.

Beverley wasn't in the living room and hadn't come to the door when I knocked. Elton John's "Nikita" was playing from the stereo, and her cat was lazing on the arm of a sofa, its tail dangling off to the side, swishing and flicking, as it eyed me with disinterest.

"Hey, kitty-cat, any idea where your mistress is?" I asked, not daring to step too close. Witches' familiars were precocious creatures, or so I'd been told. They were beholden only to their owners, and although the cat looked supercute and harmless, I knew there was possibly a terrifying monster hidden beneath all that fluffy adorableness. The last thing I wanted was to have my face torn off. In response to my question, the cat yawned, showing off its sharp teeth, and flicked its tail in the direction of the hallway.

"Good talk!" I said, giving it a thumbs up as I walked toward the hallway. When I reached past the kitchen, a sauce was bubbling on the stove and an enchanted knife was slicing and dicing up vegetables. On the window sill, a roll of bread was cooling off. I wished my food would cook itself.

"Bev? It's Dianna. I'm here for my lesson!" I called out as I walked down the hallway, passing by the bathroom and a vacant guest bedroom.

At the farthest end of the hallway, a door opened and Beverley poked her head out. She was dressed in a silk robe and her hair was wrapped in a fluffy towel, eyebrows raised all the way to her hairline. "Oh, shoot! I knew I was forgetting something." She grimaced, padding toward me.

"Dianna, dear, I apologize, but I forgot to tell you that I am hosting a little dinner for Destiny and Dawn's birthday, so we have to cancel today's lesson," she explained, referring to the twin witches who ran one of my favorite boutiques, The Midas Touch.

"Oh, that's okay. I guess I'll…go watch the live performances at The Drinking Hole or something." I shrugged and prayed that the smile on my face did not look as forced as it felt. I had no plans for the rest of the day because my lessons with Beverly could sometimes go on for hours.

If the Drinking Hole got too boring, there was a biker bar on the outskirts of town that was more my speed. I had a friend from Beckford whose band performed there every other weekend; he could keep me company. Drake and April, my two friends who were now dating, were doing their own thing—*again*. In hindsight, I should have known that there was something going on between those two. April had suddenly started wearing scarves with every outfit, and Drake, the notorious player, had stopped accepting offers from all the vampire groupies who threw themselves at him wherever we went out. The fact that he was choosing to feed only from blood bags or directly from April herself was a big deal. Coming from Drake, that was as good as putting a ring on April's finger. This was why I hated dating within friend groups. Now, I felt like the unwanted third wheel and constantly second-guessed myself when I wanted to call them and ask to hang out.

"Oh, you'll do no such thing." Beverley caressed my cheek, her eyes sparkling—like, *literally* sparkling with magic as she gave me an impish smile. "I think I have found the perfect match for you, and the two of you are having your first date this evening. So, you'll take your little butt back home and start getting ready."

"Sorry, you found my what now?" I choked on my spit, my heart doing this weird thing where it skipped a beat and then started thudding at an unnaturally quick rate. It had somehow slipped my mind that I'd asked her to set me up with someone. In my defense, almost two weeks had passed since then, and Beverley had never even indicated that she'd started the search. There were no questions about the type of guys I was attracted to, what I wanted out of a relationship, my goals—you know, all the stuff you'd ask someone before setting them up on a date with a potential life partner. "Who is he?" I demanded.

"You know the rules." Beverley shook her head. "I won't tell you anything except where you'll meet him for the date. But trust and believe that I would never put you in harm's way…unless you've changed your mind about this?" She narrowed her eyes at me.

"Of course not. Where is the date?" I gulped. Now that the day was here, the very real possibility that I was about to meet my soulmate scared the living daylights out of me. What if I was not what *he* wanted out of a partner? I mean, I was the biggest slob I knew, I had very little ambition, and the way I dressed…

What if my date showed up expecting to meet a Disney princess and got Wednesday Addams instead? Some people took one look at my clothes, the multiple piercings, and heavy eye makeup and decided that I was either one mental break away from an asylum or a single arrest away from being locked away for good. "Trouble with a capital T" was what one of my ex's mothers had called me once when she thought I wasn't listening. That's why I usually stuck to dating bikers or rock star wannabes. Well, when I bothered dating at all. When was the last time I'd even been on a date…?

"That is not the look of a woman who is ready to meet the love of her life. What's wrong?" Beverley squeezed my arm.

"Nothing is wrong," I replied too quickly, backtracking when my boss arched her brows and gave me a hard look that told me she didn't buy it.

Shoulders slumped, I sighed in frustration. "It's me, I'm what's wrong. I mean, looking back at all my past relationships, the common denominator—the one to always call an end to the relationship—has always been me!" I blurted, thumping a fist on my chest.

"So, you think there is something wrong with you?" Beverley asked, leading me to the kitchen and ordering me to take a seat at the dining table. While she poured us both some juice, I started to unload on her. Thoughts I'd never dared to say out loud because I believed that if I did, then that would make them truer than they already were.

"There has to be. Every time things start going well, I start nitpicking. I look for trouble where there isn't any and I sabotage the relationship. Who does that?" I huffed in frustration, toying with the stud on my nose. "It's not like I come from a broken home or anything. I've been surrounded by healthy relationships all my life. My parents are approaching their fortieth wedding anniversary and are still as stupidly in love with each other as they were when I was young. My grandmother has been dead for almost ten years, but I've never seen my grandfather so much as make heart eyes at another woman, and lord knows more than one matronly bible thumper in his church has tried to put the moves on him. So, what's wrong with me? Why can't I make my relationships work?"

"The easy answer would be that none of the guys you dated before were your person. Subconsciously, you knew that and put the kibosh on it before things went too far," Beverley suggested. She flicked a hand and the utensils that had been flying around us, preparing what looked to be spaghetti, stopped and settled themselves in the kitchen sink.

"I'll never get used to all this magic," I uttered in awe. "So, what's the not-easy answer? Do I have a hidden trauma I don't know about?" I was only half-joking, but a part of me wanted a straight answer from someone else's perspective. Someone who didn't live with my thoughts 24/7 like I did.

"That's for you to find out, now, isn't it?" Beverley

answered with an enigmatic smile. "But what I can tell you—and I hope you don't take any offense—is that you seem to have an inferiority complex when it comes to your family. You think you don't shine as brightly as they do, don't you, dear?"

Beverley's observation was a bullseye shot right through the heart. I actually flinched back from her words. And yet, I found myself asking, "What makes you say that?"

Beverley shrugged. "Just what I've noticed since you started working for me. The way you talk about them versus the way you speak of, and see, yourself. Your parents, the great philanthropists of Mystic Cove, your uncle, the mayor, and your grandfather— Well, let's not talk about him." She waved a hand and screwed her face up. "And then there's your siblings. Mirabelle is quickly becoming a respected figure in her field, James the hotshot lawyer, and I hear that Juno has scouts from all over the country attending her matches. You, on the other hand, are stuck working for minimum wage at a small-town bookstore."

"You forgot Dion," I croaked, smiling and trying to pretend that Beverley hadn't just flayed me alive and exposed me to the elements.

"Your brother has talent for sure, but I am undecided as yet whether it will take him places. My point, Dianna, is that you see all the good in everyone in your family except yourself. You think of yourself as the black sheep of your family, hence the armor you don every day." She waved a hand at my outfit. "Not that there's anything wrong with the way you dress, but you are well aware of the prejudices people immediately form about you the second they see all the chokers and piercings and tattoos. You think it makes it easy for them to write you off while you hide behind that sorry excuse. But the truth is—" She reached her hand across the table and covered mine. "—you are every bit as special and talented as the rest of the Flowers family. I have seen your art. Even Landon has been waxing poetic about it. He says you could make it big if you just take that leap. The question is, why don't you?"

Her question settled like a rock in a still lake. For as long as I could remember, I had always viewed myself as a lump of coal compared to the glittering diamonds that were the rest of my family. Or rather, a more apt comparison would be a weed among the bright and beautiful blooms of Flowers.

"That took a dark turn." I chuckled uneasily, not wanting to confront the truth of what Beverley had just said. "So, about that date…" I changed the topic and tried to get her to spill more details.

CHAPTER 5

"*D*on't you have friends for this kind of thing?" Dion's voice carried from my phone, perched on my dressing table. I walked back from my floor-length mirror, took a seat on a small chair, and re-positioned the phone so that I could see his face better.

"None of them are picking up and I really need a sound opinion on my outfit," I replied distractedly, applying mascara to my lashes. Dion snickered at the face I made as I tried to avoid poking myself with the mascara wand.

"And you couldn't call Juno or Mirabelle? Or the legion of chicks you're always hanging out with? You really expect me to believe that none of your friends answered their phones?" he drawled, disbelief coloring every word out of his mouth.

"Juno has a big mouth, and I don't feel like facing an inquisition from Mom about my date. And all those people at the bar are casual friends at best. April is the one I've known for the longest, but she's… It doesn't matter what she's doing now. Are you sure that jeans and a crop top are okay? I really think the dress would have been better." I looked over my shoulder at the pile of clothes littering my bed. The skin-tight, little black dress I wanted to wear for the date lay at the very top of the pile, beckoning to me.

"If you want to flash the entire town while riding on that ridiculous scooter of yours, then go right ahead." Dion shifted on his bed, shaking the phone for a second before his ridiculously chiseled face came back into focus. He was lounging on his bed, his head nestled among a plethora of pillows. His blond roots were starting to show at the roots of his dyed black hair. I could spot the damage caused by years' worth of dyeing through the phone.

My hair used to look as dry and brittle as his from the constant coloring and was only now starting to return to normal since I'd started using potions to change the color whenever I wanted. For the last seven months, though, I'd chosen to go with my natural honey blonde instead of constantly switching up the color.

"You have a point." I sighed and picked up three tubes of lipstick—one pitch black, the other blood red, and the last one a deep midnight blue. "Which one?"

"Definitely blue," Dion answered. "Not that I want to dissuade you or anything, but are you sure a blind date at the *cemetery* is a good idea? It sounds like a *Dateline* episode waiting to happen to me. Why can't you meet this guy at a cafe or any other place with living people?"

"Beverley assured me that I would be quite safe. And you know she wouldn't set me up with a psycho."

"Unless she wanted revenge on our grandfather and is using you to get it," Dion pointed out as if that was a natural conclusion to come to. "You don't know that she wouldn't do it. They've been beefing for what, a hundred years?" he added when I gave him a bemused look.

"Granddad's not that old," I said, running the lipstick over my lips. "And their beef has nothing to do with us.

Besides, setting me up with a serial killer will ruin her rep as the best matchmaker in town. But I'll send you updates as proof of life if that'll make you rest easy."

"A name would be nice. And if you can snap a picture of the guy, that would make me feel a whole lot better about letting you go off on a graveyard date." Dion muffled a yawn behind his hand.

I rolled my eyes at him; "It always creeps me out when you act like a protective older brother. In my head, we're practically twins."

"Except that I'm eleven months older. You should get going if you don't wanna be late. And remember to tell the dude to wrap it up if the date goes *too* well. We don't want Dad to burst a vein if you get knocked up by a no-name loser who works for minimum wage."

"As opposed to getting knocked up by an heir to a Fortune-500 empire?" I shot back in an acerbic tone. Dion's smile was wide and goofy in response to my unimpressed glower.

"I mean, he wouldn't mind all that much if you landed yourself a rich sugar daddy. At least that way he'd know you were set for life. On second thought, I think he might die of mortification if you brought home a dude as old as he was and introduced him as your *lover*." He emphasized the last word breathlessly, then snorted like a pig as he died laughing.

"You're so gross, and I have to go." I cut the call off before my brother spewed out any more disgusting suggestions. Finishing up the rest of my makeup, I fluffed out my hair and went to check myself out one last time in the mirror and frowned at what I saw.

I'd tried to go for a demure, understated look for this date and achieved the exact opposite. Maybe I should have gone for a lighter palette with my makeup. The faux leather jeans and bustier crop top were a little much too.

Oh, well. It's his loss if he can't handle the real me. There's no point in trying to present myself as something I am not...as something less, I told my reflection. Running my hands down my top, I nodded in satisfaction, threw my leather jacket on, grabbed my phone and bag, and was off.

~*~

The beautiful scenery of the town whipped past like a blur. The vibrant reddish browns and oranges of the drying leaves against a backdrop of the evergreens as I approached the mountain that wrapped around one side of the town in the distance were muted from behind the visor of my helmet. Fall was finally here. I could almost taste the pumpkin spice in the air. I wondered when Jumpin' Beans was going to debut their fall menu. I'd have to stop in and ask on my way back home. I couldn't wait for Halloween season next month. The stream of costume parties and the Halloween Music Festival where Dion's band would be performing. And, of course, it would give me an excuse to draw crossover art of my favorite fictional characters, not that I needed one.

I made it to the cemetery in record time. The sun was just dipping over the horizon, creating a lot of long shadows over the narrow dirt road, so I needed to have my headlight on. I was kind of regretting not taking a cab. I was pretty sure that showing up with helmet hair was some sort of first-date faux pas.

Driving past the church, I spotted some cars parked out front. I wondered what extra church activity was going on there. When I was a kid, I thought my grandfather's only job was to stand at the church altar on Sundays and preach to the masses, occasionally officiating weddings, but as I grew up, I realized he was at the church almost every day. I still didn't know what he did most days, though.

When Beverley told me that my date would be waiting for me at the cemetery, I'd wracked my brain trying to come up with an inkling of who I could be meeting. In my head, I conjured up a fantasy version of Andy Biersack waiting for me at the gates with a bouquet of black roses or spider lilies.

This wasn't my first time having a date here. As a matter of fact, I had my first kiss behind the mausoleum at the very back where the founders of Mystic Cove are supposedly buried. Oddly enough, that lucky boy had born a striking resemblance to Andy Biersack; maybe that's why I expected someone like him to be waiting for me at the cemetery gates when I parked my scooter. I certainly didn't expect the white-haired beauty standing awkwardly at the gates. He stood tall and slim and so pale that for a moment I thought he might be an apparition. A guardian of sorts. Given that we lived in a town saturated with magic and all sorts of supernatural creatures, ghosts haunting the local graveyard certainly wasn't much of a stretch.

I was so caught up in my own delusions of who my match could be, in all the chaos of rushing from Beverley's cottage to get ready and second guessing this entire match-making thing, it slipped my mind that Mystic Cove's resident zombie lived here.

I'd never met him before. No, that was wrong. He looked really familiar. His sharp jawline and almost effeminate features did nothing to detract from his handsomeness.

"You're the dude from the movies!" I blurted, snapping my fingers when it finally clicked where I'd seen him from.

"Pardon?" He blinked in confusion, stepping away from the gate and walking toward me.

Hanging my helmet on the handlebars of my scooter, I met him halfway. "I saw you at the movies during the *Resi-*

dent Evil marathon. You left right after the first movie," I explained, resisting the urge to squirm under the full effect of his pale eyes. His irises were almost completely white, but flecks of blue twinkled in and out of sight and a blue outer ring surrounded his irises. I'd never met anyone with such a disconcerting gaze. The fact that his thick-rimmed glasses magnified his eyes did not help at all.

"Oh, I think I remember you now. My name is Parker, Parker Smith. You're my date?" It was difficult to glean any emotion from him, except that he was shy and uncomfortable. Was it because I was not who he was expecting to show up, or was he a shy person in general?

Parker definitely wasn't what I was expecting. I'd seen zombies before on a wild road trip with my brother and his band, so I knew they weren't the man-eating monsters everyone made them out to be. Still, the zombie clan I'd met before had an air of danger and mysticism about them, kind of like vampires and werewolves and some witches did. Parker Smith was giving me mild-mannered, hot-nerd vibes.

He was wore a light blue shirt, a navy-blue V-neck sweater, chinos, and black Vans. It was hard to tell whether he was Clark Kent-ing it; you know, making himself appear as this adorkable harmless nerd when he could actually mess you up with just a tap of his finger.

"That would be me, Dianna Flowers." I grinned and held my hand out for a shake like this was a business meeting. Parker's hands were cool to the touch, but they all but engulfed mine. His grip was soft, his coloring almost marble against my olive skin. The corners of his lips kicked up, his eyes crinkling with silent laughter.

"Dianna Flowers?" He eyed me skeptically, lingering on the studded choker necklace around my neck and the piercings along both my ears.

"I know, right? I've been told that my name doesn't fit with all of this." I waved a hand down my body.

Parker's eyes widened in alarm, dropping his hand from mine like I was toxic. "I'm so sorry, I didn't mean to insinuate that there was something wrong with the way you look. Q-quite the opposite, in fact; you're way hotter than I thought you'd be. No, wait! That sounded disrespectful." He mumbled something to himself, adjusting his glasses and going all adorably bashful on me. "What I meant to say was that you're very beautiful. Beautiful and deadly, kinda like an oleander flower. And the goddess you were named for, Diana, or as the Greeks call her, Artemis. So, I guess your name fits you after all. Not all flowers are pretty ornaments to admire. Most can really mess you up... And I'll stop talking now before I embarrass myself even more..." He trailed off, looking everywhere but my face. Our eyes met for a split second before he ducked his head and stared at his feet, letting out a self-deprecating chuckle.

I wasn't one to melt into a puddle of goo at the sight of cute stuff like puppies, but that whole tangent Parker went on had me feeling like I was a marshmallow that had been left alone in the sun too long. I broke down in a fit of giggles, fanning my face because I could feel it heat it up. Parker's eyes jerked up to my face with an expression of wonder and fascination.

"I've never given much thought to my name and whether or not I liked it, but after hearing that, I have a new appreciation for it," I told him. Did the world suddenly shine a little brighter when he smiled? No, it must have just been the fireflies floating around in the cemetery behind him.

"That's pretty," I commented.

Parker followed my gaze. "I like to think they are spirits who've not yet crossed over, come to keep me company. Shall we?" He held his hand out to me and led me through the gates when I took it. A thrill of anticipation zapped through me and settled gently in my gut and set the butter-flies aflutter.

"Can you see them? Ghosts, spirits, and the like, I mean?" I asked, failing to quash my curiosity down. Besides, we were going to get to know each other anyway. And this was just one of the many things I wanted to know about my hand-some zombie, I justified to myself.

Parker tripped over his feet, nearly taking us both down to the leaf-covered ground. We both reached out at the same time and grabbed onto a headstone belonging to one Valerie Thompson.

"Sorry," Parker apologized. "I didn't expect you to come right out and ask about stuff pertaining to my…condition." He set his glasses straight before reaching a hand out as if to brush my hair out of my face. Unfortunately, I beat him to it.

"You mean the fact that you're a zombie? You can say it, you know. I won't run away screaming." I started walking toward the trailer house at the very back since I assumed that's where we would have our dinner.

That bewildered look of fascination came over him again. "You'd be the first. Most everyone thinks that I'll pounce on them the instant I get them in my crosshairs. You should see the look on the cashier's face at the grocery store when I buy my groceries and there's meat. You'd swear I was going to eat it raw with how green she always looks."

The resentment and anger in his voice tugged at some-thing within me. Granted, I'd known Parker for all of five minutes, but it was clear that day that the man was a cinnamon roll, sweet as they come.

"Are you talking about Gloria? You don't need to take it to heart. I'm pretty sure she looks at everyone that way. The woman doesn't have a kind bone in her body." Total lie, I didn't know for sure whether Gloria was perpetually bitter to everyone, but she never looked happy to see me and handled my stuff in a rough manner, so maybe her disdain for Parker was nothing out of the ordinary.

"If you mean the hawk-faced woman with the Karen haircut, then yes. That's her." With his hand barely touching my back, he led me down the path leading to his house. The trailer house was located across the plot of land where the Founder's mausoleum had been erected and stood under the umbrella of a ginormous yew tree. "And no, I can't see ghosts or interact with them, but sometimes I can feel their presence. There were some in my previous clan who could communicate with the dead and perform other sorts of magic." His tone was bitter as he spoke of his clan. I wanted to ask him what prompted him to leave his community, but felt it was better to bite my tongue.

"Beverley tells me that necromancy is a forbidden art amongst most witch covens. But from what I know, death magic is the only kind zombies can use. Does that put your clans in conflict with the covens?"

Parker shot me a startled look, his smile crooked and making him look younger than his years. I assumed he was in his late twenties or early thirties at most—or, at least, that was how old he'd been when he died—and he wasn't that much taller than me, five-eleven or so to my five-five.

"Death magic and necromancy are technically not the same things. In all necromantic magics and rituals, there is death magic, but not all death magic is necromancy, so there is nothing intrinsically wrong with our magic," he explained as we cleared the grounds allocated for burials and entered the small plot of land where his house sat.

"Oh wow!" I gasped at the beautiful dinner setting on the picnic table to the side of the house. The external lights were switched off to keep the moths and other bugs away, three table lanterns were set as the centerpiece of the table, and a string of multicolored fairy lights hung off the branches of the yew tree and attached to the side of the house. Fireflies flitted about and some settled on the branches, the roof, and the ground. "You didn't need to go to so much trouble. Pizza and beer while leaning against Bob Thomas's headstone would have worked just fine."

"Much as I'd like to take credit for the setup, it was Beverley who did all of this. She came by earlier and set everything up and cooked up a bunch of food for us. I can take your jacket and put it inside the house if you like," he offered when I took it off, but I declined. The temperature would drop soon and I wanted it and my phone near me.

Parker asked me to sit at the picnic table while he brought out the drinks and food. He turned down my offer to help him, claiming that I was a guest, but I had the feeling he wasn't comfortable with me stepping into his house just yet.

The leaves rustled above me, creating an ambient melody that mixed in with the crickets chirping somewhere in the distance. The cemetery smelled of wet earth and grass. I knew that a lot of people associated graveyards with heartache and loss. The way some of the graves had been left unattended for too long, it must have hurt the nearest and dearest relatives to come back very often. But there was peace to be found here too. My lips relaxed in a ghost of a smile as nostalgia crept in. Back in high school, I would sneak out of my room and come here alone, without any of my friends. Just me, a sketchpad, my phone, and earbuds. I would sit by my grandmother's grave, my back leaning on her headstone, and sketch. Sometimes I would talk to her and complain about my life like a typical teenager. Other times I would walk through the graveyard, reading the epitaphs on the headstones, mostly from decades ago, and make stories up in my head about the lives of the people buried there and make sketches of what I thought they looked like.

I was startled out of my daydream when I felt something bump into my ankles. "Where did you come from?" I smiled at the ginger kitten that head-butted my leg and peered up at me with its yellow-green eyes inquisitively. It let out a kittenish mewl and rubbed its head against my boot.

"You don't look like a stray," I commented on its shiny coat of fur and the collar around its neck. It was plump and well fed. "Can I pick you up? You want cuddles and pets?"

"If you do, she's not going to leave you alone for the rest of the night. She's quite the attention hog, that one. I hope you don't mind non-alcoholic wine. I'm not much of a drinker." Parker placed a tray with a bottle of wine, two glasses, and a charcuterie board on the table.

"That's fine with me. I have to drive the scooter home. Is she your pet?" I picked the kitten up and placed it on my lap, huffing out a laugh when it immediately curled up into a ball and purred like a truck as I scratched behind its ear.

"Kibble takes offense to being called a pet. She's more like a roommate who makes me pay for everything, gives me nothing but grief, and expects me to be grateful that she has deigned to grace me with her presence," he replied with a rueful twist of the lips, pouring wine into both of our glasses and taking a seat on the bench on the other side of the table across from me.

"So here we are." He cleared his throat, his smile growing awkward and tight. Parker fidgeted with his hands like he didn't know what to do with himself before reaching for his drink and almost drinking it in one gulp.

"Nervous?"

He cleared his throat again. "Yeah. I've never been on a blind date before and I haven't been on a 'normal date' in years, so I don't quite know what to do or say. Aside from

bringing out the main course after we're done with this—"
He waved a hand at the charcuterie board. "—or so Beverley
tells me."

"Then tonight, we'll simply eat and get to know each
other. No expectations beyond that, no pressure, okay?" I
raised my glass for a toast, and although there was hardly
anything left in his, Parker picked his glass up and tapped it
against mine.

"No expectations, no pressure," he repeated.

CHAPTER 6

No expectations. No pressure. Although we'd agreed on that, it was difficult not to have any hopes or not feel the weight of this date on our shoulders. After all, this wasn't a simple date with a guy I found on Tinder. We were here because a matchmaking witch thought we would make great lifelong partners for each other. Of course there would be a certain amount of pressure and exaggerated expectations coming into this.

I thought I was doing a great job of hiding my nervousness from Parker, babbling on about my job at the Book Coven and teaching art to kids on the weekends, but he had clammed up on me. Sure, he made all the right noises while I talked, but I could see the gears turning in his mind. He was overthinking everything and couldn't bring himself to relax, and it hadn't even been thirty minutes yet. Letting out a despondent sigh, I dropped a half-eaten cracker and made a show of checking the time on my phone.

There was a text from Dion, no doubt his response to finding out that I was on a date with a zombie. I'd sent him a text earlier as requested and never bothered to check his reply when it came through.

"Is something wrong?" Parker enquired, catching my eye before his gaze darted away again. His white hair glinted like moonlight in the fading light of day. The soft, silken strands brushed across his forehead and the collar of his shirt in the evening breeze. He kind of reminded me of Jack Frost from *Rise of the Guardians.* "Dianna?" He frowned when I didn't answer.

"Nothing's wrong per se," I hedged. "I was just wondering if maybe we should do this another time. Maybe someplace neutral so that you're not so...wound up," I said after searching for the right words to fit his mood. Parker went pale, which was saying something considering he already looked like Casper the friendly ghost.

"Wh-what? Why? Are you not having fun? Or is this just your way of trying to let me down gently?" The questions poured out of him in a torrential rush. He reached out his hand, presumably to grab mine, but he tipped over the bottle of wine, sending it splashing all over the table and dripping down onto my lap.

I yelped, jumping to my feet to avoid getting soaked and forgetting that Kibbles was still napping on my lap. The kitten let out a shrill yowl, landing on its feet before stalking away in a huff, tail and head held high.

Parker started to rush to my side and jerked to a stop, his head swiveling from the mess on the table to his house. "I am so sorry! Maybe I should go and grab a cloth or something? I don't want your clothes to stain. Do you need to use the shower—"

"Breathe, Parker, breathe!" I cut him off before he worked himself into a frenzy. I didn't think he was breathing at all. The outlines of thin bluish veins were visible beneath his skin, spidering across his neck and face. It was both disturbing and ethereal.

He took a moment to calm himself down before excusing himself and rushing into the house to grab a cloth. "Are you sure you don't want to take a shower?" he asked as I wiped myself down.

"It's okay. This wouldn't be the first time I came home reeking of booze… Though, I suppose non-alcoholic wine doesn't classify as booze. Are you okay? For a moment, I was scared you were going to pass out on me."

His eyes flashed with shame and wariness, his irises reflecting the multicolored fairy lights. His pupils were a kaleidoscope of color and a treasure trove of mysteries I wanted to unravel—if he would let me.

"I didn't mean to freak out on you, but when you suggested that we take a rain check, I was scared I'd lost my chance before we really even got started."

"You haven't," I assured him in a soft whisper and gave his arm a gentle squeeze. His gaze locked onto where my hand was wrapped around his arm. Despite his slim and lithe figure, there was solid muscle definition under his sweater, which led me to believe that he was not averse to working out. "The only reason I said what I said was because I could tell you were not one hundred percent into this. I thought maybe I was intimidating you or something." I debated whether to say more, but at the end of the day, we were trying to build a relationship with each other. That meant we needed to learn to be honest with our thoughts and feelings. "I am aware of what people have been saying about you and how they've been treating you, and I don't think I'm wrong in assuming that the town's reception of your arrival is why we never see you much around town. This is your safe haven." I gestured to the house and the graveyard in general. "It must be stressful to let someone you hardly know around the one place where you feel completely at ease. That's why I think maybe we should have done this on neutral ground. There are tons of places where we could go that are private and require no socializing with anyone but the two of us."

"Oh, I don't want you to leave, though. I was stuck in my head because all of this, all of *you*, seemed too good to be true. I kept waiting for the other shoe to drop, for you to realize that you'd rather be anywhere else with anyone else than here, with a zombie reject."

"Good thing I'm the queen of rejects then, and us rejects gotta stick together. Unless you're a closeted psycho serial killer or some kind of pervert, I don't care what you are, Parker. What I care about is what's in here." I stepped up to him and splayed my hand on his chest. His heartbeat picked up, but it was still slower than mine. So, zombies had a slow heart rate. You learn something new every day. The cheeky thought flitted through my mind before I got distracted by the feel of his pecs beneath my fingers. So firm and...well, muscular for a guy built like a beanpole. It wasn't until Parker cleared his throat and wrapped his hands around both my wrists—I guess somewhere along the way, I started to use both hands to feel him up—that I realized what I was doing.

Flushing, I tried to step away from him and only managed to take a single step with his hand around my wrists. "Sorry about that. I didn't mean to molest you. You're just...uh...sturdier than you look." Was that my voice? An octave higher than usual and embarrassingly breathy? Since when did I sound like that?

Parker's eyes twinkled with mirth, his smile a perfect balance between boyishly bashful and sinfully sensuous.

"Let's take a walk!" The idea popped into my head out of nowhere, but upon more thought, a stroll around the cemetery was just what Parker needed to relax and get out of his head. Mindless fun like going dancing or getting drunk would be better, but this would have to do for now, and I said just as much when he hesitated and brought up the dinner that waited for us in his house. "It can wait, unless you're really starving."

He shook his head. Again, the urge to run my fingers through his hair overcame me. I laced my fingers through his instead and started leading him toward the mausoleum on the other side of the burial ground. "Tell me about yourself," I hummed conversationally, leaning into him just a fraction.

"What do you want to know?"

"Hmm… Your age, for starters." We paused to watch a squirrel scurry past in front of us and disappear beyond the wrought iron fence that circled the perimeter of the graveyard.

"I'm twenty-seven," was the short response from Parker before falling silent again. A flare of irritation shot through me that he wasn't making any effort to keep the conversation going. In his defense, my question did not elicit much by way of response, but he could have followed up with a question of his own. Swallowing my annoyance, I tried again, this time injecting a bit of levity into my tone. Lips curled in an impish smile, I bumped my hip against his. "And how long have you been twenty-seven?"

I was rewarded with one of those pig-like snorting laughs. "A *Twilight* reference? I didn't peg you as a fan." He ran the pad of his thumb across my knuckles.

"Oh, please! A movie filled with angst-ridden, edge lord vampires and a main character with questionable decision-making skills? *Twilight* and the *Vampire Diaries* were my jam back in the day. I had posters of Edward and Damon Salvatore all over my room. Not to mention all the books and merch," I supplied, sounding mighty proud of myself.

Parker shook with laughter. "But you would have been, what…ten, eleven when the first movie came out. How did you get caught up in all the hype?"

"Nine, actually. And my older sister Mirabelle was a teenager at the time. It didn't take much to drag me into all the vampire mania that was going around. So, are you gonna tell me how long you've been twenty-seven or not?" I eyed him from the corner of my eyes.

"Zombies are not like vampires, Dianna." He paused in front of a black granite headstone and crouched down on his haunches, brushing his fingers across the name engraved on it. Two vases stood on either side of the stone, the white lilies in them dried and withering away. "We don't stop aging when we're turned. That means I have been twenty-seven for—" He paused, executing a short mental calculation. "—seven months now. My birthday is on the third of February."

"Ah, an Aquarian then. I'm a Gemini, by the way. I turned twenty-three on the sixth of June." I sat down on the grass and leaned my back against one side of the tombstone. Parker did the same, knees bent and propping his hands on them.

"So, you guys age, then?"

Parker nodded, lacing his fingers together. "Up to a point, or so I'm told. I was changed when I was seventeen, after being in a car accident. And I've been growing at a normal rate into adulthood since then. According to my former clan leader, the aging process should start crawling to a snail's pace when my body is at its physical peak—usually some-where between my thirties and forties."

"Can I ask you how you came to be as you are?" I asked cautiously. Because I had all my attention focused on him, I caught the slight pinching of Parker's features and the way his Adam's apple bobbed up and down on a swallow. "You don't have to tell me about it if you don't want to." I gave him an easy way out if he needed it.

"No, it's not like some epic secret or anything. Just a couple of bad memories." He tipped his head up to look at the evening sky. The warm red and orange hues of the sunset were giving way to the night sky. The stars were starting to come out and winked at us from above as the faint outline of the moon peeked through the wispy clouds. He took a steadying breath, and when he spoke, his voice was detached, as if the things that he was speaking of had happened to someone else.

"When I was seventeen, my family and I were going home after watching a college football game in Minneapolis. My older brother was playing and his team won that day, so after the game, we all squeezed into my dad's Ford—my parents, older brother, my two little sisters, and I. Dad was going to treat us to a meal at a steakhouse. The mood was still pretty high and rowdy in the car, everyone speaking over each other." His tone was wistful, his eyes distant, and a sad smile graced his lips. "We never saw the other car coming. Right as we pulled off the freeway, some idiot was trying to overtake us when he really shouldn't have and crashed headfirst into our car. Sent us into a tailspin before the car rolled over a couple of times."

A gasp lodged in my throat. Now I wished I hadn't asked anything at all, not if he was going to tell me that he lost his family in that accident. What did you even say to something like that? "Parker—" I croaked.

"We all made it out alive." He looked down at me, the expression of pained amusement telling me that he knew the thoughts that just ran through my brain. As quietly as I could, I let out a quiet breath because I had no idea what I was going to say when I opened my mouth.

"Karl, my older brother, he, my mom, and I came off the worst. We were in the hospital for weeks—various broken bones, organ damage, and all sorts of contusions. Luckily, the accident wasn't career-ending for my brother."

Something about the way he said that had me sitting up straighter, my ears perking to attention. "And what about you?"

"I was no superstar athlete, if that's what you're asking." His chuckle was without humor. "But that accident... Yeah, that was pretty much the end of my life as I knew it. Somewhere between the accident site and the end of my stay at the hospital, I must have come into contact with another zombie's blood or body fluids."

"Is that how...zombie-ism...is that a word? Is that how it's transmuted?" Yet another thing I'd never been able to find out. I asked the zombies I met with my brother, but they had all been closed-lipped about it.

Parker dipped his head in a jerky nod and wrapped one hand around the opposite wrist. Despite the carefully blank expression on his face, the chokehold on his wrist betrayed his emotions. "Yeah." He paused to clear his throat when his voice cracked. "John, my...uh, my former clan leader, told me that the change happens when another zombie's DNA gets introduced into your bloodstream. It had to have been someone at the hospital. A nurse or doctor."

"A blood transfusion?" I asked, remembering that way back in the day, various diseases, even AIDs, could be contracted through a transfusion. But I thought that hospitals were really careful about that stuff now.

Parker shook his head. "No. Our blood would never pass a blood screen. But it had to have been done deliberately. I don't know who or why, but there are some sick people out there, so who knows."

I nodded but couldn't shake the fear of some crazed psychopath out there turning people into zombies.

"So...I died...sort of," he said. "I flatlined. Everyone thought I was dead. But it was just the zombie blood taking over my body. They even did the whole embalming thing, but I guess they couldn't flush out the zombie blood, not that they knew they needed to. But eventually the zombie blood took over and I woke up. At my own funeral."

I let out a curse. I couldn't help it. It was like something out of a horror novel.

"Yeah, that was how many of the people who had come to pay their respects responded, even my family. After the initial shock wore off, they were happy to have me back, but..."

He paused to collect himself. I gulped, waiting anxiously for the rest of the story but not wanting to rush him.

"The changes in me happened gradually," Parker went on. "My hair bleaching, the photosensitivity, the accelerated healing, and this...sixth sense of mine. Sensing spirits and such. My family didn't know what to make of it, and neither did I."

Parker leaned his head against the headstone, closed his eyes, and sucked in a shaky breath. I scooted closer to him and forcibly pried his fingers from around his wrist. A bluish, almost purple bruise in the shape of his fingers was impressed on the skin he'd been gripping so tightly. I have no idea what made me do it, but I laced our fingers together and brought his wrist to my lips and kissed it.

Parker jerked, his eyes snapping open. "What was that for?"

"It's called comfort. Get used to it." I leaned into his side, laying my head on his shoulder.

"Oh." Slowly, I felt him relax as he laid his head on top of mine.

I couldn't imagine what he—and his family—had been through. Whenever someone dies, how often do we wish and pray we had that person back? His family got their son and brother back, but then… They must have been so confused, so frightened. And Parker, to not know what was happening to him.

I have no idea how long we remained in companionable silence after that as the world turned dark around us, with only his house providing some light. And even that didn't illuminate much beyond the picnic table. I was thinking of suggesting we finally have that meal when Parker spoke up once more.

"The change wasn't quiet and restful, not on me or my parents. I was sick, a lot. And the doctors couldn't tell what was wrong with me. Some days I was moody and quiet, others feverish and in so much pain that I would lash out. I was never a violent person, but there I was, throwing stuff against the wall, ripping my bedsheets with my bare hands. It didn't help that all my senses were dialed to eleven. I couldn't stand to open my eyes during the day, and the quietest sounds felt like a gunshot going off right next to my ear. My parents were at their wits' end by the time John found us."

"Your clan leader? How did he know about you?" My brows furrowed in suspicion.

"One of the doctors at the hospital was a warlock. He never consulted on my case personally, but I guess he must have picked up on what was happening to me and called the local zombie clan leader. Needless to say, none of them believed what he was saying at first. My dad threw him out of the house, thinking he was a scammer trying to make a quick buck off our situation. But he left me his number and one night when the pain got too much, I called him and he showed me how to deal. He introduced me to others like me, told me of this whole other fantastical world of magic and things I'd only ever read about or seen on TV.

"Eventually, I accepted what I was, and when I did, I tried to get my family to see the truth of what I was as well and stop living in denial. That didn't work out the way I pictured in my head. To paraphrase my father, he'd rather I was dead than have an undead freak of nature under his roof. So, I left." He shrugged nonchalantly, but there was something off about the way he moved.

"Parker, I'm so sorry," I whispered.

He shook his head and wrapped an arm around me. "Don't be. Life happens and I've learned to deal with it, despite being thrown on a thorny path. I put the pain and everything else firmly in my rearview mirror and things are finally looking up for me," he said meaningfully, his look warming me up from the inside.

There was still so much more I wanted to know, but I had to remind myself that this was only the first date, and we'd have more time for heart-to-hearts in the future. Besides, his stomach chose that moment to growl like a bear straight out of hibernation, so I laughingly suggested we make our way back to his trailer and our waiting dinner.

CHAPTER 7

"Are you sure you're not a vampire? Your steak looks like it could jump off your plate and run away at any moment," I teased Parker when I got a good look at his steak. I didn't even think it was cooked with the way it was bleeding all over his potatoes when he sliced through the chunk of meat to give the kitten a bite.

"I haven't heard that joke before." Parker rolled his eyes before digging into his meal, moaning in pleasure when he got a taste of Beverley's potatoes drenched in garlic butter sauce and a plethora of other herbs and spices. The sound he produced deep in his throat was low and sensual. Who knew watching someone eat could be such a turn-on?

"Beverley is a goddess in the kitchen. I can't remember the last time I had a meal this good," Parker exclaimed with a goofy smile pasted on his face.

"I'm inclined to think she's a goddess, period. Maybe I should ask her to give me cooking lessons too," I mused, segueing into telling him all about the potion and spell crafting lessons I was receiving from my boss. The walk earlier went a long way to easing Parker's nerves, and though there was still an air of melancholy about him after telling me about how he got turned into a zombie and everything that transpired with his family. But he was more relaxed and easier going than he'd been at the start of the date.

Conversation flowed easily between us as we exchanged anecdotes about our jobs; his stories about working in a funeral home beat mine by far. Even though he sounded content with his life the way it was, I realized that Parker was hardly living at all. It sounded like he only associated with a handful of people and rarely went into town unless it was to meet his friend Emil or run some errands.

"Since I came to your place for our first date, the next one's going to be on my turf," I told him when he walked me back to my scooter. I had Kibbles cuddled in my arms, her purrs vibrating against my chest, making me feel a little sleepy.

Parker arched his brows and I would like to think he was blushing at the implication that I was already looking forward to a second date. His voice laden with sarcasm, he said, "That doesn't sound ominous at all. What did you have in mind?"

Biting down on my lip, I debated telling him or just springing our next date as a surprise so that he didn't spend time between now and then coming up with reasons to bail on me. He looked like the type to make plans on a whim while feeling confident and then his introversion kicking in later, making him regret making social plans.

"How do you feel about live music? There's a club, more like a bar, really. Not the biker bar one I told you about, this one is geared mostly to a vampire clientele," I quickly added before he gave me an answer. "Humans are allowed though, and they always have these up-and-coming bands performing over the weekend. I was thinking you could come with…" I stopped walking and stood in front of him so that I could look up into his eyes. His aversion to being seen out in public was written clearly across his face, but I had no intention of letting him back out of this.

"I know you're not comfortable with being around other people, but like I said, the bar will be filled ninety percent with vampires who won't bat an eye at having a zombie in their midst. And the ten percent of humans there are guys and girls just like me who are into this stuff." I might have pouted a little and given the puppy dog eyes. I wasn't beyond using my feminine wiles to get him to say yes.

Parker's lips trembled. At first, I thought he was upset, but then he let out a bark of laughter, startling Kibbles in my arms. He flicked my nose before taking his kitten from my arm. "Don't say 'people like you' as if it's a bad thing; I happen to enjoy your company immensely."

"Does that mean you'll come with me?" I bared all my teeth in a wide grin.

Parker nodded. "As long as we take my car because there's no way we're both going to fit on that death trap of yours." He flicked his chin in the direction where I'd left my scooter.

"Awesome. I'll text you the details soon. Oh, that reminds me…" I took my phone out of my bag and held it out to him. Parker entered his phone number and I immediately called him, letting his phone ring three times before cutting it off. "That's my number. You better save it. And thanks for tonight, Parker. I really enjoyed this." I waved my hand, encompassing the entire graveyard.

"So did I," he whispered, stepping closer. So close that even with the paltry moonlight and the weak light from the lamp sconces on either side of the cemetery gate, I could pick out the flecks of blue in his near-white irises. He was within kissing distance, and although I told myself that I wasn't going to rush anything, I knew I would let him do it. So long as Parker was the one to make the first move, I would allow myself this one moment of pleasure.

The world seemed to fade away. The only thing I was aware of, other than Parker's extremely kissable lips, was my heart pounding furiously in my chest. I could probably charge up a small power plant with how it was racing. Parker's tongue peeked out as he licked his bottom lip, and I unwittingly let out a sigh. He moved, leaning his head down and we were almost there…until the roaring of a car engine ruined the magic. Like a mirror shattering, the heady atmosphere broke apart around us and reality intruded. The chirping crickets sounded a little louder and the smell of grass stronger as we jumped apart and both looked across the road at the sedan that had apparently been parked there this whole time without either of us knowing. The car pulled onto the deserted road, its tires skidding against the dirt as the driver gunned the engine.

"What the—" I started to curse as the driver sped past the streetlamp, illuminating his face for a split second, but I was cut off by the agonized noise coming from Parker.

He took a single, dazed step forward and stopped, his eyes glued onto the sedan as it disappeared down the road. He was slack-jawed, eyes wide and brimming with too many emotions to count. Amongst those emotions was dread. His pupils were dilated, making it seem as if his eyes were pitch black instead of white, and his mouth kept shaping words I couldn't make out, but no other sound escaped him.

"Parker, what's wrong?" I reached out to grab his hand, but he slapped it away and flinched back from my touch as if I had shocked him. I hissed out in pain, clutching my hand close to my chest.

"Oh no! I didn't mean to do that. I'm so sorry, Dianna. Did I hurt you?" he gasped, taking my hand in his and rubbing his thumb on the top of my hand. He was trembling, I realized, but I don't think Parker noticed it until I held his arm in place and gave it a reassuring squeeze.

"Hey, talk to me. What has you so spooked?"

Kibbles jumped down from his arms and squeezed herself between his legs and rubbed her head against his shins to comfort him. Parker shook his head. He shrugged off my touch and dug the heels of his hands into his eyes. "I thought I saw…" he started, whispering so quietly, I struggled to hear what he was saying as he shook his head again. "It's nothing. I just didn't expect there to be a car parked there. It scared me, that's all." He tried to reassure me with a smile, but it was completely wooden and didn't reach his eyes.

"Thanks again for tonight. I'll see you for our next date on…Friday, right?" he asked with fake cheer, practically pushing me toward my scooter. And just like that, our incredible date ended on a weird note.

CHAPTER 8

"So?" Beverley demanded first thing Monday morning when I walked into The Book Coven with our daily breakfast orders. I snorted at the hungry gleam in her eyes that wasn't for the box of muffins or cups of coffee in my hands.

"So?" I shot back, dumping the food, my bag, and my jacket on the counter.

Beverley rolled her eyes and nabbed herself a freshly baked blueberry muffin from the box. "Don't make me deck you first thing in the morning. How did the date go?" She took a huge, obnoxious, slurping gulp of the coffee and swore when she burned her tongue.

"Wow, Bev, I didn't know you were that invested in my love life. You know I don't kiss and tell," I drawled, enjoying the way her eyes narrowed, the left squinting more than her right in irritation.

"I could always compel it out of you, you know?" She raised her hand, purple sparks coming to life at her fingertips.

"No, you won't," I said around the huge bite of muffin in

my mouth. Beverley was too much of a sweetheart to violate my privacy like that. It would not only ruin our professional relationship, but the friendship and the mentor-mentee relationship we'd built since I'd started working with her. Taking pity on her, I decided it wouldn't hurt to drop a kernel of information to keep her satisfied for the moment. "I won't tell you what transpired, but I will say the date went well enough that there will be a second one this Friday." Except for the last bit when Parker freaked out on me after seeing the car, I'd classify the date as a success. We'd been texting each other all weekend, and I'd even convinced him to go on a "not date" with me Sunday morning—coffee and a stroll in the park.

My lips curled in a sneer as I remembered all the curious attention we'd garnered and how people practically rushed to get out of our way when they saw Parker. More than that though, I wanted to make Mystic Cove truly feel likc his home. I wanted everyone to accept him because there was only so much a person could take. What if Parker one day decided he'd had enough and skipped town?

Should I have been scared that I was already attached after only meeting him twice? There was definitely some chemistry between us, but that didn't mean I was ready to throw myself headfirst into a relationship. With my short attention span when it came to romantic relationships, the real challenge was whether I'd be able to stick it out for the long term.

"Hah! What did I tell you? This old goat is never wrong when it comes to matters of the heart," she exclaimed, slapping her hand on the counter. "That's all I needed to know. Now, finish up your breakfast and get to work, those shelves won't restock themselves."

I spent most of the day with a cheesy smile on my face and rolling my eyes at the smug smirks from Beverley when she caught me smiling off into the distance. When my lunch break came, I grabbed my stuff and stepped out to meet Greta downtown, where she was going to show me the place she'd scoped out. I wasn't going to make it back in time for my afternoon shift, so Beverley gave me the rest of the day off.

The address Greta had sent me was in a quaint neighborhood called Sunnyside, near the sea but not as expensive as Beachside—which, as the name suggests, was by the beach and mostly a string of vacation houses for the wealthy who only came into town during the summer.

She and the real estate agent were waiting for me in front of a two-story, blue-gray, bungalow-style house. Although it was two stories, the bungalow was the smallest one along the row of houses that lined either side of the road that wended past the neighborhood, up to Beachside, and ending on a stretch of beach.

"Oh my gosh, that's so cute!" Greta gushed over my scooter, having jogged down the driveway to meet me. "I should totally get myself one. That would help me save the cost of taking public transport all the time and give me wiggle room to start saving for a car."

"I can hook you up if you want. I know a dealer who won't rip you off," I offered, automatically responding to her enthusiastic smile with one of my own. She had a Julia Roberts smile, beautiful and infectious, like getting a burst of sunlight injected directly into my bloodstream.

"So, this is the house?" I asked, hanging my helmet off the handlebars of my scooter.

"It is, and the living room and kitchen come fully furnished. Three bedrooms, so if we wanted to cut down on our share of the rent, we could get a third roommate as well. Is that cool with you?"

My mind immediately went to Parker, but I threw that

idea out the window. He had a good thing going with his whole setup at the graveyard. And even if he wanted to move in, what would our neighbors say? I glanced around the quiet neighborhood. Everyone would be at work or school by now, but I could easily picture the ruckus that ensued during the weekends. Dads mowing the lawns, dogs barking from the backyards, and children kicking a ball up and down the sidewalk.

"I don't have a problem with that. Shall we?" I gestured to the house

The agent gave us a tour of the house, and like Greta said, the living room was fully furnished. It was all secondhand but in better condition than the stuff I had in my apartment. The appliances were all older models except for the washing machine, which looked relatively new. There was a stove but no fridge. I mentioned that I could just bring mine until Greta and I could afford to get a bigger one. The first floor consisted of the living room that opened up into a small dining room, the kitchen, and a single bedroom, and upstairs were the two other bedrooms and the bathroom.

"The landlord doesn't mind if you guys want to paint your rooms or get small renovations done, so long as you run it past him first," the agent told me while Greta peeked out the window of the master bedroom. It overlooked the backyard; a single tree stood out there, covering our yard and branching across the fence into the neighbor's. The lawn was dry and overtaken by weeds, but a backyard meant that I could get a puppy if I wanted. Which I didn't, because, you know, I was a cat lover. But it was nice to know that if I moved in, I at least had the option.

"So, what do you think? It's a steal for such a great place, right?" Greta beamed at me, leaning on the window sill. She'd obviously fallen in love with the bedroom—with the whole house in general—but I didn't mind handing the master bedroom to her and taking the second biggest bedroom, which was across the hall.

"It is. I can't help thinking that it's almost too good to be true and I'm wondering if there's a catch." I speared the estate agent with a pointed look. He was a stocky man in an ill-fitting suit. His complexion was blotchy despite the day's weather being pretty mild, and I was pretty sure that squirrel-looking hairdo of his looked that way because he was wearing a toupee.

"Ah…" He gave a nervous chuckle, taking out a handkerchief and dabbing at his forehead. "Well, you see… There was an incident last year, and no one has really wanted to buy the house. The landlord had to bring its rental price down twice. I'm only telling you because, well…you're a vampire." He shot Greta a nervous glance. "And I don't know what you're supposed to be," he went on, looking at me, "a witch? Anyway, I figured you wouldn't mind living here since your kind lives with the paranormal every day," he blubbered.

Greta and I exchanged uneasy and confused glances. "What incident?" Greta probed, standing beside me. The estate agent wiped his forehead again, turning even redder than he already was. He mumbled something under his breath that we didn't catch.

"Come again?" I leaned in closer.

"There was a murder! A man killed his fiancée and her lover when he caught them in bed together. It caused a huge ruckus in town about a year and a half ago. Now the neighbors claim the house is haunted and that they sometimes hear the dead fiancée crying in the master bedroom."

Greta startled at that, looking around the empty bedroom as if the dead woman's ghost would pop out at any second. I did the same, but I was looking for signs of blood spatter.

"How am I only just hearing of this now?" I wondered. Secretly, I thrilled at the possibility of living in a haunted house. Now, I know how these things end up in horror movies, and I've laughed more times than I'd like to admit at those memes making fun of dumb teens in said horror movies, but this was a once-in-a-lifetime opportunity. Besides, the ghost sounded more like a depressed ghost than a vengeful one. And we had witches coming out the wazoo; any of them could perform an exorcism for us if need be. Heck, Beverley could teach me and I could do it myself.

Clapping my hands together and rubbing them in anticipation, I turned to face a green-looking Greta. "I'm sold. How about you?"

She scratched her head. "I mean, it's better than all the places I've looked at already, and it's a short commute to work, but I'm so not sleeping in this room." She shivered, rubbing her hands up and down her arms.

"So we switch," I said, more than eager to get to know my ghostly roommate. "When can we move in?"

The agent promised to send us the lease agreement before the end of business the next day and rushed off to his next appointment. With nothing left to do for the day, I debated heading to the funeral home and surprising Parker. Maybe I'd even get to watch him work on a corpse. But as Greta and I made our way down the driveway, I remembered what my granddad said about reaching out to her. She was, in a way, just like Parker. Relatively new to town and stumbling about, trying to set roots here. And what's more, she was a newly transitioned vampire.

"Hey, I got nothing else to do for the rest of the day. You wanna catch a movie or something?" My brain totally stalled on what else we could do for fun. It was too early in the day to head out to any of the bars, but I guessed catching a meal together would work just as well.

"I'd love to, but I have to get to work. Maybe next time?" She toyed with the straps of her handbag and gave me a shy smile.

"How about this weekend? I'm planning on hitting the club with some friends. You should join us. There'll be live music, booze, and the best nachos you'll ever have." I wiggled my eyebrows. I knew that it was technically supposed to be my date with Parker, but I was going to introduce him to Drake and April then anyway. This was me, killing two birds with one stone—spending time with Parker and expanding his, and Greta's, social circle.

"I never say no to tacos. You can text me the details," Greta said, her smile somehow expanding even wider.

CHAPTER 9

My plan to surprise Parker at work was a bust. His boss, Mrs. Graham, told me it was his day off and he was probably chilling at home. Considering that I would have known where he was if I'd just called or texted him, I should have done exactly that instead of driving my scooter down the road to the cemetery, but hey, I was passing by there anyway. A quick stop just to check if he was home couldn't hurt.

Music blared from the front windows of the house. His blinds were drawn shut and the front door was left ajar, but only because he had a screen door. I let out a huff of laughter when I recognized the song playing—Eminem's "Space Bound." Raising my hand to knock on the door, I hesitated when I heard Parker's voice. It was difficult to make out what he was saying with all the music, but now I felt guilty for showing up just like this. What if he had company and didn't want to be disturbed?

While I was debating whether to let him know I was there or not, Kibbles made the decision for me. I didn't notice her pop her furry little head through the pet door until she was already pouncing on me and I let out a yell of surprise, landing on my butt when I lost my balance on the stairs that led up to Parker's front door. The music paused and seconds later the screen door opened as Parker peeked his head out. His confused smile melted into a cocky grin when he saw me.

"Just couldn't stay away from me, could you? Whatever happened to waiting 'til Friday for our next date?" He leaned on the doorframe, arms crossed over his chest. His very naked chest.

Parker was dressed only in a pair of gray flannel pajama pants that rode low on his hips, showing off the V-shaped ridges that disappeared below his waistline and the trail of fair hair that led to…

Shaking my head, I forced my eyes up to his face and away from his gorgeous, ripped—albeit pale as milk—body. Not that it did anything to lessen the frying synapses in my brain from seeing him half naked. He was not wearing his glasses today. His eyes were glazed over, heavy-lidded, and bloodshot. His hair was a mess, as if he'd just rolled out of bed. Parker Smith was a hot mess—in the best way. In the "I want to rip my clothes off and plaster myself all over him" kind of way.

"Dianna?" His eyes sparkled like he could follow the path my thoughts were sailing down. That cocksure smirk was like a smack upside my brain and allowed me to pick my metaphorical jaw off the floor and my butt from the ground. And then I remembered that I heard him speaking to someone inside—and he was dressed like that. The reminder was like being doused in a bucket of ice-cold water.

"I got off work early and thought I'd come watch you do your stuff at work, but your boss told me it was your day off. I'm not interrupting anything, am I?" I tried to peek into his house, past his lanky frame, but couldn't make out anything except for a shiny stainless-steel fridge nestled between the kitchen cupboards.

Parker shook his head. "I was just uh… You're not interrupting anything." As if I would believe him when guilt was written all over his expression.

"Oh? I thought I heard you talking to someone. Were you on the phone?" The logical part of my mind warned me to stop interrogating the poor guy.

"Oh, that. I was just having a chat with one of my neighbors. They like to pop in to say hello once in a while," he replied with an embarrassed grin. It took me a moment to understand his meaning.

"I thought you said you couldn't talk to ghosts!" I exclaimed.

"The communication's practically one-sided. I do all the talking and they just sort of blow a cold breeze down the nape of my neck or give me shivers down my spine. I'd like to think I'm well versed in translating the meaning behind each chilling response," he deadpanned, stepping back from the doorway and motioning for me to enter. His house was not at all what I expected.

Parker came across as the type of guy who liked everything in its place, neat and tidy. But his living room was exactly what you'd expect from a single dude in his twenties. Dirty dishes in the kitchen sink and discarded cartons of Chinese takeout on the counters. On his coffee table were two cans of Monster energy drink and a half-empty bag of salt and vinegar chips.

"Wow, you're such a guy!" His living room took up most of the space in the front of his house, with a kitchenette squeezed into a corner. He'd gone for the bare minimum when it came to furniture. A love seat—not even a full couch —faced a fifty-five-inch plasma screen TV mounted on the wall while two beanbags were tossed haphazardly around the coffee table.

The most impressive thing in his living room was the video game setup. Parker owned both the latest PlayStation and Xbox gaming consoles and a top-notch surround sound system. To the right of the front door was what looked like a computer gaming setup. Next to it were two portable shelves, one filled with books and the other with games, CDs, and vinyl records. To the left of the wall where his TV was mounted was a second door that probably led to his bedroom and bathroom. My nose twitched when I caught a familiar scent in the air, but for the life of me I couldn't place it.

"I wasn't aware that I'd ever been anything else. Can I get you something to drink?" he asked, walking toward the kitchen, leaving me to take off my boots and place them next to his discarded sneakers.

"Do you have beer or wine?" I asked over my shoulder as I went to the bookshelves, my eyes skipping over the collection of games and novels and straight to the trio of picture frames on the middle shelf.

"Afraid not. Your options are milk, orange juice, energy drink, soda, and coffee. Oh, and there's water," he called out.

"Soda it is then. With ice, if you have any," I replied distractedly, all my attention on the pictures. One of them was of his family; I could tell even without Parker pointing it out. An older, dark-haired woman stood between two boys who looked so alike you'd think they were twins. She had Parker's smile, his features—the sharp jawline and high cheekbones, the slash of her eyebrows and the lush chestnut brown hair. Or rather, Parker had his mother's features. The boy to her left, his older brother, had harsher features, more masculine compared to Parker, but one glance and you could tell that they were brothers. Like his hair, Parker's eyes were a different color in this picture, a vibrant electric blue instead of the almost white with blue flecks he bore now. He was so young in the picture, early to mid-teens, I guessed. And standing in front of them were two blonde girls who could have been anywhere between ten and thirteen. All of them wore wearing football jerseys, and Parker's older brother was smeared in war paint. The picture must have been taken before or after a game. Since he wasn't in the picture, I assumed Parker's dad was behind the lens.

The next two pictures were taken years later, after Parker became a zombie, and judging by the light-haired people in the photos with him, it must have been after he joined a clan. One was with an older man around my dad's age, his toothy smile aimed at the camera with his arm thrown around a petite, short-haired girl. The picture had been taken right as she was rolling her eyes, a reluctant smile on her face and her arm wrapped around Parker's midriff. He was doubled over, laughing his butt off. The second photo was just the two of them. Parker stared down at the girl and she up at him with a look I could only describe as love. Something bitter and ugly twisted in my gut. I shoved it down.

I sensed him coming to stand behind me. Without looking at him, I asked, "Have you ever tried contacting your family since you left?"

"Once. It didn't go how I'd hoped, so I never bothered them again. Here's your soda." He handed me the glass, took my hand, and led me to the couch.

"And the other people, are they your clan mates?"

A muscle ticked in his jaw. "Yeah." That was it. That was all the answer I got.

He picked up the TV remote and switched it to some random channel before excusing himself and disappearing past the second door. I flipped aimlessly through the channels, but my attention kept drifting back to the photos. Who was that girl? I knew what love looked like. I saw it in the way Dad looked at Mom. Parker looked like he was madly in love with that girl. Where was she now? What happened between them? Did he come to Mystic Cove because they broke up? Curiosity burned me, but I wasn't sure that I had the right to ask him anything. He came back three minutes later with a shirt on—thank goodness—and plopped down next to me.

"So, what do you want to do for our third date? Play at being a couch potato with me?" he asked, tossing a journal that had been stuffed under the couch's armrest onto one of the beanbags. Loose sheets of paper flew out from between the pages, but Parker barely gave them a second glance, leaning back on the couch, legs spread wide and all his attention on me. This was such a contrast to the shy dork I was used to, I didn't know how to handle it.

Tucking my feet underneath me on the couch, I threw my hand over the couch's back and started to tell him that this didn't count as a date when the blunt tucked behind his ear caught my attention. "No way! You smoke weed?" I gasped, snatching it from him before he could react. So that's what I smelled earlier. "Do zombies get high?"

I knew vampires and some shifters had to tweak their drugs and alcohol if they really wanted to get a buzz going. April and I once smoked a joint from Drake's personal stash and it nearly laid us out for the entire weekend.

"We do. I don't smoke often, only when I need to decompress and silence my thoughts for a little bit," Parker replied in a subdued tone.

"And you needed to silence them today?"
He nodded.
"Do you want to talk about it? I'm a great listener."
"Thanks, Di, but maybe next time. Today, I just want to not think about anything but getting high as a kite, stuffing

my face with junk food, and rotting my brain with TV and video games." He mirrored my seating position on the couch, his eyes roaming all over my face. "And now that you're here, my day's only gotten that much better." He leaned in close, his eyes flicking down to my lips when I bit down to stop myself from smirking.

"Is that so?" I smirked, leaning toward him as he shifted to get closer to me. I could feel my heart thrumming in my throat, my blood singing in my veins, and my body humming with nervous anticipation. Gulping down the lump in my throat, I wet my lips and my eyes fluttered closed. I could all but taste Parker's lips on mine and we hadn't even kissed yet.

I waited and waited for a touch that never came. Instead, I felt Parker's mint-scented breath brush across my face when he let out a shaky sigh. For whatever reason, he chose not to go for the kill and gave me a feather-light kiss on the tip of my nose and took the blunt from me to light up with a lighter he grabbed from the coffee table.

"You any good at video games?" he asked after taking a puff and passing the joint to me.

I took a hit and coughed at how potent it was. This was definitely a strain designed for vampires and the like. One hit and I could feel a buzz building beneath my skin and tension I wasn't aware that I was carrying melted away. "Depends, what do you got?"

Parker leapt off the seat and dragged the two bean bags in front of the TV. We spent the rest of the day beating the crap out of each other while passing the blunt back and forth between us.

When the munchies hit, the only thing I wanted to eat was a meat lover's pizza. Parker claimed he was too blitzed to drive to the pizza place and almost choked on his saliva when I pointed out that ordering delivery was a thing. But his reaction was nothing compared to the expression on the delivery guy's face when he showed up at the front door.

Like he'd wanted, the day passed in a haze of smoke and mindless fun as we went from playing games to marathoning *Game of Thrones*. So many times throughout the day, there were moments when I would think to myself, *This is it. We're finally going to kiss.* Parker had certainly grown bolder with his exploring touches, and I was practically sitting on his lap as we watched *Game of Thrones*, but then he would get this pained look in his eyes and pull himself back.

At some point late in the afternoon, halfway during the first episode of the second season, I drifted off to sleep. My head lay on his lap and his arm was curled around me, his fingers drawing figure eights on the exposed sliver of my stomach from where my T-shirt had ridden up. His touch was both oddly arousing and soothing and I would have drifted off to la-la land with a smile on my face if my eyes did not drift off to those photographs again.

Was she the reason he was so gun shy with me?

CHAPTER 10

The line to get into Club Sanguine was daunting, as usual. Even before the three of us exited the taxi, I felt the bass of the music reverberating in my chest. Fixing the strap of her blouse, Greta stared at the line snaking down the block in awe and then at the flashing neon sign overhead with the club's name and the logo of a cocktail glass with red liquid most likely meant to be blood.

"Whoa! I feel a little underdressed," Parker joked, adjusting his beanie and, like Greta, taking in the patrons lined up outside. Most of them were vampires from in and around Mystic Cove, and since the club liked to advertise itself as a den of vice and debauchery, the dress code pretty much reflected that. The skimpier and sexier, the better. Mesh shirts, leather, chains, and studs were some of the bolder choices, while the older vampires who longed for bygone times or just wanted a bit of dramatic flair went with modernized Victorian and Regency era-inspired outfits— billowing pirate shirts and corset tops. I'd gone with a front lacing corset, leather shorts, and chunky thigh-high boots. I'd advised Greta to wear pants; a lot of the guys there tended to get handsy after knocking back blood-laced booze.

"You're fine as you are, don't worry." I curled my hand around Parker's and leaned into his side. In fact, he was more than fine. Dressed in a black and blue Linkin Park shirt, denim jacket, ripped jeans, and converse hightops, he looked like he'd stepped straight out of a magazine spread. I still couldn't get used to seeing him with blue eyes. He'd left his glasses behind and wore specially designed blue-tinted contact lenses. Parker said the lenses irritated his eyes, so he didn't wear them for prolonged periods. I couldn't decide whether I preferred him with or without the glasses.

"Are you sure we'll manage to get in before the night is over? It looks like the whole town showed up tonight," Greta questioned as we stepped onto the sidewalk. She started to walk to the back of the line, but I grabbed her wrist with my free hand.

"Stick with me, kid, and you'll never have to suffer Club Sanguine's never-ending lines ever again."

I led them both to the very front, snickering at the confused glances she and Parker exchanged. As it turned out, the two of them knew each other through my grandfather, so that saved me the awkwardness of acting as a bridge of friendship for the night.

I felt like a celebrity at the front door when the bouncer let us in on sight, and I might have preened and bragged a bit that I knew the owner's son when Parker and Greta asked me how I did it.

"I can get both of you on the pre-approved list if you want. That way if you ever want to come here without me, you don't have to bother waiting in line with the plebeians," I shouted to be heard over the music. It was worse inside than outside, my entire body vibrating to the rhythm of the song playing. Parker winced and, belatedly, I remembered that he said he had sensitive hearing. I assumed that he was able to adjust that little bit of blessing/curse like the vampires who crowded the dancefloor, but maybe I should have asked instead of assuming.

"Plebeians! Listen to you, sounding like a queen!" A familiar voice laughed from behind us. Drake walked out from the crowd to join us, a devil-may-care smirk on his face and his pants tighter than Khloe Kardashian's latest nip-tuck. He pulled me into a bear hug before stepping back to assess my friends.

"You're new; I haven't seen you at any of the coven gatherings before," he said to Greta. "And you must be the infamous zombie dating my best friend. Allow me to introduce myself—Drake Haas at your service." He bowed gracefully, kissing Greta's hand and giving Parker a firm handshake.

"Ignore him. He likes to think he's a thespian, but he's just a drama queen, only good for drinking his weight in blood and wine." I jabbed him in the ribs with my elbow, saving Parker and Greta from any more of his theatrics.

"And I'm also the reason you never have to wait in line like plebeians at this or any of my father's establishments," he said mockingly. "Now, I'm sure we have a lot of catching up to do, but why don't we move somewhere a little less noisy. April's waiting for us."

We followed him up to the level above the dance floor that was surrounded by soundproof glass. We could still see and hear what was going down on the dance floor, but the lights and noise were muted and not so headache-inducing.

"Your friend feels old—like, *really* old—and powerful too," Parker whispered in my ear, his hand brushing up against my backside as he guided me up the stairs. I could have told him that Drake could hear him even with the whispering, but I knew he wouldn't say or do anything to embarrass me.

"He is, but don't ask him about it. He hates being reminded that he's a fossil compared to his twenty-four-year-old girlfriend."

"I can hear you, Petal!" Drake called over his shoulder, giving me the middle finger.

"I know you can hear me; that's why I said it," I shot back, my lips twitching. This was a common play-by-play between the two of us, so Drake knew I meant no insult with the age quip, and I knew that he wasn't really mad.

"Petal!" I didn't have time to brace myself for the spiky and pink-haired pixie that came barreling toward me. April knocked the wind out of me as she wrapped her arms around me and buried her face into the crook of my neck. "I feel like I haven't seen you in ages," she gushed, almost choking me out until Drake pried her away.

"Petal?" Parker raised his eyebrows, a small smile on his face at the nickname.

"Ignore it. They think it's cute and that I won't follow through on my threats if they don't stop calling me that," I replied. Drake and April called me Petal because of my last name and because it annoyed the heck out of me. I was as far from a delicate petal as you could get. My boyfriend, however, thought differently—the traitor!

"I think it's cute. I think I'll start calling you that now."

April's attention snapped to him as if she had not noticed his presence until then. "Oh, wow, aren't you a cutie? The zombies we met last time were really intense, but you look like you should be in a mathlete club or something. I'm April Choi, by the way, Dianna's oldest and bestest friend. We went to high school together, so I know everything there is to know about her, including all the embarrassing stuff she probably won't tell you."

"Alright, that's enough. How about I get a few drinks into me before you start dredging up my dark past." I squeezed myself between April and Parker and quickly introduced Greta. The five of us went to the table that Drake had reserved for us, and the conversation and jokes flowed around as freely as the drinks. I noticed Parker stuck to nursing a single beer instead of knocking them back like the rest of us. Surprisingly, Greta was a tank. She and Drake both had strong thresholds for hard liquor and were engaged in a drinking battle.

"Are you a lightweight, Parker? You've hardly touched your drink," April pointed out, a shisha pipe in her hand as she blew out pink smoke.

"Someone has to keep an eye on this one. Wouldn't want her to start stripping again," he joked, referring to the anecdote April told earlier about the first time we got drunk and I thought I could seduce the boy I had a crush on at the time by giving him a strip-tease in front of everyone at the party.

I scowled at him, but his response was to lean down and steal a kiss. Parker might not have been as buzzed as the rest of us, but he was more laid back than I'd ever seen, soaking in the atmosphere and the company. A coil of apprehension I wasn't even aware I was carrying loosened within me. It was important to me that Parker got along and meshed into my friend group seamlessly.

"So, Parker, how did you choose Mystic Cove as your home? It's a far cry from Minneapolis," Drake asked, stealing the pipe from his girlfriend and inhaling.

"Uh… It's an embarrassing story." Parker laughed nervously, scratching the back of his neck.

"That's the best kind! Spill, mister," April egged on, clapping her hands in excitement. Parker's gaze flicked to me, begging for help.

"Please, do tell. I want to know why I've never heard this embarrassing tale," I said haughtily, loving the alarmed look he got at being put on the spot.

Groaning, he slumped back in his seat. "I was sort of wandering around with no destination in mind after leaving the clan," he started. "At some point, I ended up in Boston, broke and no one was hiring, so I thought I'd resort to pick-pocketing. It was going to be a one-off thing, just to get enough money for a meal and a bus ticket to anywhere else but Salem."

He paused to collect himself, taking a long swig of his beer. I was on the edge of my seat, sure I was about to hear something unexpected.

"I thought I found the perfect mark, an old man drinking alone at a bar. When he left, I trailed him. Long story short, I got whipped pretty good. Turned out, the old man was former special forces."

I frowned, wondering why the story sounded familiar to me. Then it hit me. "Wait a minute! You're the punk who tried to rob my grandfather?"

At my exclamation, Drake snorted out his drink through his nostrils from laughing so hard. I remembered my grand-father visiting Boston for church business a while ago and telling us he'd nearly been mugged.

"Sorry?" Parker chuckled.

"So, you're now dating the granddaughter of the man who convinced you to come to Mystic Cove," Greta said thoughtfully. "Small world."

"It's a small town," I said. I guess after having lived here my whole life, seeming coincidences didn't surprise me much. Bev would say there's no such thing as coincidences—only magic.

After getting enough drinks in us, we headed down to the dance floor when the band started preparing the stage so that we could get spots right up front.

"Are you enjoying yourself, mister shut-in?" I asked

during the band's set as they serenaded the club with one of their love ballads.

"Surprisingly, yeah. I can't remember when I last let my hair down like this, and I like that your friends accepted me just like that." He put one of his hands around my waist and snapped his fingers.

"Well, one of them is a vampire, so…" I shrugged. "I'm happy that you're having a good time. I was scared this would be too much stimulation for you." I couldn't stop smiling or playing with the silky strands of his hair. And as much as I was having fun, I couldn't wait to take him home. The way this night was going, it could only end one way—with both of us getting our minds blown. As if he could read my thoughts, Parker's eyes went dark, the sensual promise gleaming in them making my toes curl. I let out a gasp, my eyes fluttering closed when he leaned down to kiss me. I wet my lips and waited to feel his on mine, but his touch never came, and Parker was taut as a rope in my arms.

"What's the matter?" I asked, opening my eyes to see his dead gaze fixed at a point over my shoulder. I turned to see what he was looking at, but couldn't see anything out of the ordinary amongst the sea of writhing bodies on the dance floor.

"I need to take care of something. Please, wait here for me."

He left without waiting for my reply, and I didn't see him for the next twenty-five minutes.

CHAPTER 11

I found Parker outside the club, crouched against the wall, his head tucked between his knees. He was gasping for breath and on the verge of a panic attack when he heard my footsteps approaching. His beanie was discarded on the pavement, his hair was disheveled, and his eyes were glassy with terror. My breath froze in my chest when I noticed how violently he was trembling; so much so that I was getting a headache just by seeing his teeth shatter so roughly.

"Babe, what's wrong?" The endearment slipped out on its own, but neither of us even noticed. Parker's eyes were on my face, but I got the sense that he was looking *through* me, not at me. There were ghosts in his eyes.

"Hey, talk to me. Did you find the guy you were looking for?" I asked softly, peeking over my shoulder for any suspicious characters. Nothing jumped out at me. There was still a line of people waiting to get in, but they all mostly minded their business, except to cast a few glances our way. One of the bouncers caught my eye, a questioning look on his face, but I shook my head. I didn't think we needed his help.

"Yeah, it was John," he croaked. I ran the name through my memory twice before it clicked. Parker had told me that his former clan leader's name was John, but I didn't know why Parker left the clan in the first place.

"Did the two of you have a falling out? Was he looking for you?"

I held onto him, both for comfort and to keep my balance, but I didn't think I could stay in the crouched position much longer. My thigh and calf muscles were burning from the exertion, and I could feel the tingle of needles and pins working their way up my legs.

Parker's breathing stuttered. "We didn't get that far. I forced him to leave. I…I just didn't expect to see him after all this time. It was like waking out of a beautiful dream by getting sucker punched in the face. I was finally making a life for myself here. I was starting to feel alive again…" He reached out to caress my cheek, but he was talking more to himself than with me. I leaned into his touch and listened.

"And then, boom! John shows up out of nowhere and I get reminded of all the crap in my past and I just…" He stopped himself from saying anything else.

"You just what? Talk to me, Parker. I don't know how to help you if you don't tell me what the deal is with you and this John guy. Let me be here for you," I pleaded, shifting my weight again to keep from falling on my butt.

Parker was super cagey when it came to the time he spent as part of a zombie clan. From the few snippets he'd let drop, I knew he'd been happy with them for a while after falling out with his family. But something had happened to change that.

Groaning, Parker stood and pulled me up with him, wrapping his arms around my waist and burying his face in my hair. He breathed in deep and I did the same, drawing in his scent and curling my fingers into the back of his shirt.

"I want to tell you, Di, I promise. But I'm afraid you won't want me anymore if I do."

I stiffened in his arms. That didn't sound good. Parker must have followed my thoughts because he hurried on to explain.

"I didn't break the law or do anything crazy, but what I have to tell you is pretty messed up. I don't know if it's fair of me to ask you this, but please give me some time to sort myself up and build up the courage to finally spill my guts to you."

I swallowed down the lump in my throat and squeezed my eyes shut. "Take all the time you need."

Parker pulled back, his face swathed in light and shadows that made him look like a sculpture crafted from marble. The expression he wore tugged at my heart and warmed me up from the inside with its intensity. I'd never wanted someone as much as I wanted him.

"Thank you." He whispered, leaning down. If he pulled back from this kiss again, I swore…

A gasp escaped me when his lips covered mine in a tentative touch. And then another, and another. Each kiss grew bolder and turned that bubble of warmth with me into a raging inferno of desire. Pushing up on my tiptoes, I ignored the wolf whistles coming from the line and pushed him against the wall of the club and wrapped my arms around his neck.

Parker's hands cupped my butt as he pinned me closer to him and elicited a surprised chuckle from me that ended in a wanton moan when he flicked his tongue against mine. That alone was enough to make my core tremble and turn my legs into jelly, so I allowed myself to sink into the kiss for a moment longer before pushing away so we wouldn't get arrested for indecent exposure.

"We should probably go back inside before the gang

comes looking for us," I mumbled, struggling to pry my eyes open and tasting Parker on me as I spoke.

"You mind if we call it a night? I'm not in a partying mood anymore." He cupped the back of my neck, massaging my scalp. If he was trying to calm my raging hormones, he wasn't helping at all. I nodded and quickly texted April and Greta to let them know we were heading home and to make sure that April took Greta home.

We walked down the block so that we could catch a taxi. Parker pulled me to his side the moment we sat in the back seat, and I laid my head on his shoulder, suddenly feeling sleepy.

"Where to?" the driver asked, staring at us through our rearview mirror.

Parker squeezed my side to grab my attention. "Can I stay over at your place? If I'm left to my own devices, I'm afraid my thoughts will eat me alive..." He gulped and squeezed my side again and added, "I'm scared that I might run and never come back."

I gave the driver my address and led Parker to my apartment. I was supposed to be moving into the new place the next week, but I'd yet to get to packing. My living room was scattered with all kinds of occult paraphernalia, an easel with a half-done painting, and a couple more strewn about that I was considering submitting at the gallery for a showing.

Parker arched his head back at the sounds coming from my ceiling. Pointing his finger up, he asked, "Are those—"

"Yep," I cut in, tossing my bag aside and taking off my boots. "Make yourself at home and raid my kitchen if you want. I'm going to get changed." I stepped into the bathroom to wash my makeup off and have a mini freak-out at the fact that Parker was spending the night. I doubted anything would happen, but still...

I found him paging through my sketchbook and admiring the character designs for the graphic novel I would never write. The TV was playing at a low volume in the background, and he'd poured us each a glass of wine. He'd stuck to a single beer at the club. I wasn't sure if I should be worried that Mr. I-don't-drink was having his second drink of the night.

"You're very talented, you know that? These could easily be character designs for a high fantasy video game."

"They are for a graphic novel, actually. Or a webcomic. I can never decide which because I am not as good at crafting words as I am drawing or painting. I sort of have all of these characters, some of them have backstories, but I don't have a plot," I groaned, throwing my legs on Parker's lap as I leaned back on the couch. He put the sketchbook aside and started massaging my feet. I was in blissful heaven.

"Tell me what you have so far. Maybe I can help," he offered. He'd removed his contacts while I was changing, and although sadness still lingered in his eyes, the shadows were mostly gone and he was relaxed. "What?" He bristled when he caught the skeptical look I gave him.

"Nothing. I just didn't know you were into storytelling and stuff." I stretched my hand to the table and grabbed my wine glass.

"I used to want to be a game developer when I was younger. I even managed to create an indie game when I was nineteen, and I was planning to enroll in a course that would allow me to do it professionally. Instead, I found myself stuck as a mortician. Maybe one day I'll revisit that dream," he confessed, sharing with me another piece of himself. Progress. Slow, but still progress.

I asked him to tell me about the game he built. We managed to find it on an indie game website and played it together before moving on to creating a tentative game plot based around my character designs. When we both couldn't go more than five seconds without yawning, I dragged Parker to my bedroom and tried not to choke on my tongue when he stripped to his boxer briefs before jumping into my bed and falling fast asleep.

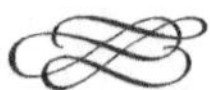

CHAPTER 12

PARKER

The compulsion to run was still tormenting me weeks after I saw John at the club. At one point, I'd started packing my bags, ready to steal off like a thief in the night and move to another state where he would never find me. Maybe even go abroad. I'd always wanted to travel through Europe. I could get there somehow. The only thing stopping me was Dianna Flowers.

The more time I spent with her and got to know her, the more she meant to me. As cheesy as it sounds, I saw forever in her eyes. I lived for her crooked smiles, sweet kisses, and…everything about her. For so long, I'd been living in a world void of color, stagnant and haunted by the past, until she showed up on my doorstep with a twist of mischief about her and a never-ending curiosity in her olive-green eyes.

I thought I'd imagined seeing John the first night I met Dianna. I'd convinced myself that it was my conscience acting up and making me relive the guilt I thought I'd finally put behind me. I was finally moving on and opening myself up to the idea of falling in love again. It wasn't a big leap to think I would hallucinate John Dobbs after all this time. After all, he'd promised to find me and make me pay for what he thought I'd done. My nightmares returning the same night as my first date with Dianna wasn't all that shocking. I was moving on, the first girl since Layla who'd stirred more than a passing interest. Layla would never get a second chance at love. She would haunt me in my dreams.

I should have known that this new life I was trying to build was nothing but a pipedream. But when I didn't see or hear from John after that initial sighting, I lost myself in the dream once more. And then it all came crashing down around me like a bloody house of cards.

I only prayed that after I socked him in the face at the club that he would stay away. Hopefully he'd hopped into his car and gone back to wherever he came from. My phone buzzed on the table. I didn't know the number, but the area code was familiar. Stifling a sigh, I rejected the call and placed my phone face down. John was calling again, as he had been since we fought at the club. Why couldn't he just take the hint? I'd left the clan like he wanted and hadn't kept in contact with anyone. What more did he want from me?

My phone started buzzing again and I silenced it, trying to focus on what Dianna was saying.

"Aren't you going to answer that? It must be important if they keep calling you back."

"It's not." My reply was short and abrupt. I didn't want to get into it with her. I knew I was walking a thin line already, keeping such a huge secret from her. Irritation flared in her eyes, which she quickly buried. I was still yet to tell her about John and Layla and why I'd left my clan. I planned to do it soon; we couldn't move forward in our relationship otherwise. The only thing keeping me from saying anything was that I was a coward; I was scared that once she knew, she would turn her back on me like everyone else had.

I thought she would push me to tell her the real reason why I was ignoring the phone call, but she hopped off my desk and started exploring the mortuary. She'd stopped by after her classes at the art school, and today was the first time I'd seen her since last weekend when Drake, April, and I helped her and Greta move into their new place and held an impromptu housewarming party. That was another gift Dianna had given me—friends.

Since our night out as a group, Drake, Emil, and I had hung out together a few times while the girls did their thing. Dianna was finally taking a chance on her art and had submitted some pieces for a showing at the gallery. Although she had pieces she could submit already, she'd spent the last two weeks in a painting frenzy. When she wasn't at work, she was holed up in the spare bedroom at her place painting up a storm. We'd only seen each other briefly in the last five days, mostly communicating via text. I'd been swamped on my side as well. The winter tourist season was starting to stir, with people passing through Mystic Cove or setting up camp for the winter, even though we were only halfway through fall.

With the influx of people coming in, we were bound to see an accident or two, but what happened had on Monday morning had been a travesty. There was a pile-up involving two civilian cars, a police van, and a delivery truck. No survivors, save for the truck driver. Mrs. Graham and I had been busy all week dealing with grieving families and preparing for the victims' funerals.

Pushing off from my seat, I walked over to where Dianna was standing, examining the refrigerated storage lockers and wrapped my arms around her. She tensed up for all of two seconds before leaning back into my chest and tipping her head to look up at me.

"Hey," I murmured, trailing my hands under her shirt, loving the silky smoothness of her skin under my hands.

"Hey, yourself." She smiled up at me and started to say something, but changed her mind. Before I could ask what was bothering her, she loosened my hold on her so that she could face me and curl her fingers into the hair at the nape of my neck. The strands brushed against my collar and I was probably in need of a haircut before I started to resemble a sheepdog. "I want to ask you something, but don't feel pressured into saying yes if you don't want to."

The first thing my mind jumped to was that she would push me to talk about my past, and I automatically started to come up with yet another excuse. But Dianna didn't wait for my answer and continued speaking.

"Come to family brunch with me." Her cheeks were pink and trepidation darkened her olive eyes. "See, my mom heard that we're dating and she's been bugging me to bring you over for dinner or brunch. I swear I tried to get us out of it, but knowing my mother, she could very well show up here and meet you herself if I don't introduce you."

I don't think she took a single breath in the time she blurted all of that out. This was new, seeing her so anxious and terrified. Dianna was a grab life by the reins type of girl. In the month and a half that we'd been dating, I'd gone into town and socialized more than in the two years I'd been living in Mystic Cove before that. She'd been helping me get out of my shell and used to being around people and I'd learned that she was not one to back out of a challenge.

While I was nervous about meeting her family—they were kind of a big deal—I wasn't sure how to take it that she seemed to want to keep me as far away from them as possible. Did they not know I was a zombie? Her mother heard about us from someone else, so was Dianna planning to keep us a secret for as long as she could? I was a bag of mixed feelings, and not all of them were good. I wanted her to show me off proudly in front of her family like she did with the rest of the town, yet I was aware of my own hypocrisy in keeping vital information away from the person I was dating.

"Do you not want me to meet them? If not, then I won't come." The words tasted rancid on my tongue. I crossed my fingers, hoping she would tell me that she wanted nothing more than to have me meet her parents. But at the same time, the thought of meeting her father agitated the nest of hornets buzzing around in my stomach.

"I do want you to meet them! I'm just afraid that they'll scare you away—my dad especially. He has..." Her eyes wandered to the ceiling, her face screwed up in a thoughtful expression. "You must understand, my father is a nice guy and I love him like crazy, but he can be a bit of an elitist. My brother Dion and I used to joke that he had our lives mapped out before we were born, except that it isn't that much of a joke."

I was beginning to glean the picture she was trying to paint for me. "So, basically, he had incredibly high standards for his children, which extends to their potential partners, and seeing as how I work in a funeral home..." I trailed off, my statement coming off as a question.

Dianna nodded. "My father has a sharp tongue. I don't want you in his line of fire." She leaned back against the lockers. I took the opportunity to cage her in and rested my forehead on hers. Standing this close to her, I was able to make out the striations of a darker shade of green in her eyes and witness the moment her pupils flared, the black eclipsing the olive green.

"Consider me forewarned. I can't promise not to call your dad out to his face, but I will gladly join you all for brunch if it makes you happy."

When Dianna perked up under my gaze, I knew I'd said the right thing. Now I just had to convince one of the most influential men in Mystic Cove that her daughter was not dating a dud.

~*~

The Black Pearl was a popular post-Church dining establishment. Dianna and I arrived before her parents and were seated by the time they and her grandfather walked in. It took at least ten minutes for them to get to us. People kept stopping them to talk about something or other. It gave me time to study Mr. Flowers and calm my nerves. From what Dianna had told me, her father was the hospital director, her uncle was the mayor of Mystic Cove, and her mother was on the board of just about every committee in town. They were like the Windsors of Mystic Cove, hobnobbing with top town officials every other week.

Mr. and Mrs. Flowers were dressed impeccably. The stones around Mrs. Flowers' neck and at her ears alone must have cost more than I made in a year, and Mr. Flowers looked like every rich, intimidating person I'd ever seen in a movie. Although his face was unlined, his hair had gone as white as mine and he had very austere features. At the moment, I could only see his face in profile, but I could see a bit of Dianna in him, from the cut of their jawlines and the shape of their noses. Finally, Mr. and Mrs. Flowers turned their attention to us, as if they'd only just noticed we were there at all.

My blood froze at the frosty glare from Mr. Flowers. If looks could kill, that one glance would have ripped me to ribbons right then and there.

Dianna placed her warm hand on my thigh. "Are you having second thoughts?" she whispered in my ear, her breath wafting across my skin.

"A little bit." My voice came out gruff and pained. I

threaded my fingers through Dianna's and held on for dear life.

"Parker, so glad you could join us today. How've you been?" Father Granger squeezed my shoulder, his smile open and welcoming, nothing like his son-in-law's. I'd almost forgotten that there would be at least one other friendly face at lunch besides my girlfriend. Father Granger liked me, despite our initial meeting.

Pushing my chair back, I gave him a handshake and a relieved smile. "I'm good, sir. How about you?"

Father Granger and I talked for a little bit as he filled me in on what had been happening at the dormitory for the underprivileged and people like Greta and me that he ran on behalf of the church while Dianna greeted her parents.

"Are you joining us for brunch?" I asked.

Father Granger shook his head. "Normally I would, but I have some stuff I need to deal with at the dormitory. I'm just waiting on my takeout and then I'll be leaving you to it."

I must have looked as green as I felt because Father Granger chuckled low and deep and whispered to me before he pulled his granddaughter into a hug. "Just be yourself, son. But don't be a doormat either, or Daniel will walk all over you."

Nodding, I steeled myself for that ice glare from Mr. Flowers again.

"Mom, Dad, this is my boyfriend, Parker Smith. Parker, allow me to introduce you to my parents, Daniel and Rebecca Flowers."

I glanced away from Dianna's strained grimace to her mother's beaming smile. For a moment, my brain stalled. I had thought that Dianna looked like her father, but on second glance, Rebecca was what Dianna would look like in three decades, right down to that crooked but breathtakingly beautiful smile.

"It's a pleasure to finally meet you, Parker. I was starting to think my daughter would keep you in the closet indefinitely." She aimed a mock glare her daughter's way. "And I'm sure she's been filling your head with nonsense. I promise that we're not the carnivorous monsters she's painted us to be." She winked.

"Mom!" Dianna groaned, covering her face with her hands and mumbling something under her breath.

"I promise I've heard nothing but good things. You've raised a beautiful and wonderful daughter. My life's all the better for having her in it." Both Dianna and her mother turned a lovely shade of pink at my words. Rebecca's twinkling laughter resounded around the room as she took a seat on the chair that her husband pulled out for her.

"Aren't you quite the charmer? Only half of what you said is true, but I can't say I don't appreciate you trying to cover for my daughter and her unfiltered mouth."

My greeting with Daniel Flowers was much more reserved. A simple handshake and a, "Pleasure to meet you, sir," and then we sat in silence—Daniel staring at me like I was a bug he wanted to dissect under a microscope while I pretended to be unbothered by said death stare. Father Granger's order was brought to our table and he excused himself, leaving us in awkward silence. A wordless conversation passed between mother and daughter.

Clearing her throat, Dianna asked, "I know why Dion's not here; what's your excuse for not inviting Jamie or bringing Juno?"

"Your brother and sister both had commitments they couldn't shirk. Did you receive my email about the curator position in New York?" her father asked, pouring himself a glass of water.

Dianna rolled her eyes. "I did, and I have no interest in moving all the way to New York."

"But you are interested in wasting your god-given talents, not to mention the degree I paid for, for a substandard job as a bookseller and for this—" His eyes flicked over to me. Fortunately for Mr. Flowers, his wife stepped in before he put his foot in his mouth.

"Daniel! We talked about this," she hissed through clenched teeth. "Can we have one meal as a family when you're not badgering the kids? Dianna is old enough to make her own decisions."

"What Mom said," Dianna deadpanned. I could only watch in silence as Dianna and her father stared each other down while Rebecca signaled for a waiter. Beneath the table, Dianna's nails dug into my hand, probably to keep herself from doing something she'd regret later. You could cut the tension with a knife between the two of them, and the rest of us were at risk of suffocating from it. Thankfully, Rebecca was a pro at navigating this specific minefield. Dianna's mother started asking me about my work and personal life. I deflected as best as I could, only telling them that my family was in Minnesota and that we weren't very close.

"I hear that Nicoletta Graham is training you to take over the funeral home," Daniel mentioned casually, the first thing he'd said to me since we sat down. So far, Rebecca and I had been keeping the conversation flowing. Dianna chimed in every now and then, but mostly pushed her food around her plate. She went still when her father started to address me.

"Ah, yes, sir." Rebecca had given me leave to call her by her first name, but I didn't want to presume that Daniel wanted the same thing. I stuffed my mouth full of shrimp tempura, unsure what else to say.

"So, is this something you want to do, or is it the only avenue available to you because of your...predilection?"

"Dad!"

"Daniel!"

Dianna and Rebecca gasped in unison, their expressions a mask of mortification. They were more offended than I was. If anything, I was amused at the veiled insult. I'd heard them all and, frankly speaking, Daniel Flowers meant less to me than he assumed, so his words did not hurt as he'd intended. I wanted to have a good relationship with Dianna's family, but if they didn't want the same thing, it was no skin off my nose. But I didn't like that he was hurting Dianna with his behavior.

"What? I'm simply asking about the boy's ambitions. I can't imagine working as a mortician pays much. Dianna may dress like she gets her clothes from the Salvation Army and live in that pathetic excuse of an apartment, but she's used to a certain standard of living, one that cannot be supported by a mortician's salary," Daniel said, feigning innocence.

"Yeah, right," Dianna scoffed, pushing her food away. "I moved out of that place, by the way. And I am not 'used to a certain standard of living.' I've been living off my own income ever since I got a job. What is this really about?" She leaned back in her chair and crossed her arms. Her jaw was clenched painfully tight and a vein at her temple pulsed angrily.

Daniel also pushed his food away and dabbed his mouth with a napkin before tossing it at the table. "I'm wondering what you're thinking dating a...a zombie." He whispered that last bit in outrage. "For goodness's sake, Dianna! We know next to nothing about these creatures, unlike the vampires and shifters. I am concerned for your safety. What if this boy wakes up one night feeling peckish and decides that you'd suffice as a midnight snack?"

A pig-like snort escaped me before I could catch myself and I miserably failed to cover it up with a cough. Wrong move.

"Do you find this amusing, Smith? I heard about why you were evicted from your previous home, about all the pets that suddenly went missing when you were living there," Daniel sneered, his eyes alight with malicious glee when my smile disappeared and I scowled at him.

"Dad—"

"I don't eat human flesh, Mr. Flowers," I said, interrupting Dianna before she could jump to my defense. "Nor do I eat cats, dogs, or any other pets that you may think of. That story you heard is complete rubbish. I wasn't the one stealing pets in the complex. A group of people who didn't want a zombie living amongst them thought it would be funny to frame me as a pet murderer and get me evicted. Their plan worked, but it was then discovered who was behind the pet-nappings, something you would have known had you simply asked me what it means to be a zombie instead of assuming the worst about a man you'd never met." I dragged in a ragged breath, but it did nothing to calm my rising anger.

"Yes, I am undead, and I have special abilities that most humans don't, but so does forty-five percent of the Mystic Cove population. And yet none of the witches or shifters or vampires are being persecuted for who they are. Not all witches are good people, not all vampires value human life. No matter the species or race, there will always be good and bad people, but at least they are given the chance and courtesy to prove themselves before being so undeservedly judged. I am a good man, Mr. Flowers, one who's been keeping his head down for far too long in this town and allowing everyone else to malign my character simply because I do not want to cause further conflict, but I find that I am growing weary of being the local punching bag."

The sound of my chair screeching as I pushed it back drew the attention of those around us in the restaurant. "I care about your daughter—deeply. Maybe you came here thinking you could intimidate me into leaving her, but the only thing you're doing is pushing Dianna away." Digging through my wallet, I took out some bills to cover my and Dianna's meals. "Thank you for inviting me, Rebecca. It was a pleasure meeting you. Babe, I'll see you later, okay?" I kissed Dianna on the forehead and gave Daniel a short nod and walked out without a backward glance.

My father was such a jerk!

"I hope you're proud of yourself," I said, trying to keep my eyes from welling up with anger. "This is the last time I'm going to say this: keep out of my life, stop trying to force jobs on me, and for the love of all that is holy, keep your bloody nose out of my relationship with Parker!"

I ignored his and Mom's pleas and rushed after Parker, wincing when I caught the intrigued expressions on everyone's faces. Within the hour, word of our altercation would spread around town, and I had a feeling that Parker was going to bear the brunt of it. The town pariah versus Daniel Flowers; no way anyone was going to believe that Dad was the one who was wrong in this situation.

Sometimes I wanted to bash these people upside the head, especially Parker's former neighbors. That was the first time I'd heard the story about the missing pets. Parker only told me that the residents of his apartment complex raised a big stink about him being a zombie and not feeling safe in his presence. I didn't know someone had played a cruel and distasteful joke, framing him for killing pets.

The top of my head threatened to explode. I was angry at everyone and everything. The black-hearted jerks who refused to let Parker live in peace, my dad, and even Parker for still keeping his cards close to his chest and not letting me in.

I care for your daughter—deeply. He'd said that to my dad, but apparently caring for me didn't mean he trusted me. Three weeks had passed since the incident at the club, and I still didn't know why John Dobbs came looking for him and why it freaked him out so much. I was losing my patience and I'd come this close to looking up Dobbs online and finding out the truth myself.

"Babe, wait up!" I caught up with Parker in the parking lot. His severe expression softened when he saw me jogging toward his car.

"What are you doing here?" He pulled me into his arms, threading his fingers through my hair.

"You didn't really expect me to stay after all of that, did you?" I got on my tiptoes and pressed my lips onto his. It was just a short, chaste kiss, and our noses brushed together; stress touches meant to cool us both down. "I'm so sorry about my dad. He's not usually such a jerk— Actually, he is, but he usually means well. That doesn't mean it's acceptable, though."

"You're not the one who should be apologizing, Petal. I probably shouldn't have run out of there like a coward, though, or went off on him. There were other ways to correct his misconceptions."

"You shouldn't have to correct anyone. It's not your job," I insisted. Parker started to retort, but I silenced him with another kiss. I got the feeling that we'd keep going back and forth otherwise. "Why did you never tell me about the pet thing?"

Parker squinted, his lips pressing into a thin line. "I don't know. I was embarrassed, or angry. It didn't seem important at the time, and it's really something I don't want to dwell on because it'll drive me mad otherwise."

"But it's important to me. You're important to me, Parker. I want you to trust me, to share your burdens, and be open with me like I am with you. I want you to stop letting them win." I stretched my hand outward, gesturing to all the people walking along the promenade.

"When will you tell me about John Dobbs? I've tried to be patient, I really have, but I'm starting to wonder if you'll ever break out of this habit of yours. I know there's stuff that's hard to talk about, or maybe something you think I won't want to hear, but know that you're setting a precedent for our relationship going forward. How would you feel if I start keeping vital information from you just because I was afraid of how you'd react?"

Pain and resignation flashed in his eyes, his throat working as he swallowed twice. "You're right, I can't keep you in the dark anymore. I'll tell you everything once we're somewhere private. Let's go home."

~*~

The drive back to Parker's place was fraught with heavy silence, both of us physically present but miles away mentally. I was terrified. Now that Parker had finally relented and was going to spill all his big, bad secrets, my stomach was in knots. He was convinced that once I knew what he was hiding, it would spell the end of our relationship, and now my mind was running the gamut, dredging up all kinds of scenarios.

Leaning my head against the car window, I started sightlessly at the scenery rushing past and ignoring the slew of messages from my mother.

Dad and I would need to talk eventually, but right now, I couldn't be in the same room with him without wanting to lay into him about everything from his relentless need to put me in a box of his liking to how he'd treated Parker today.

I was trudging silently behind Parker, my boots crunching on the grass and dried leaves as we made our way through the cemetery, so I didn't notice he'd stopped walking until I bumped into his back.

"Ouch, what gives?"

"Something's wrong," Parker whispered, going completely motionless. I started to walk around him to see what he was talking about, but he pulled me to his side. His front door had been left ajar, and the lock was destroyed. Someone had broken into Parker's house in broad daylight!

"Stay here and call the cops," he ordered, rushing into the house without any regard whatsoever for his own safety.

"Parker, wait!" Cursing when he disappeared into the house, I quickly dialed the sheriff's office, reported the break-in, and then followed after Parker.

Broken shards of glass laid on the floor from one of the front windows. I didn't even notice that it had been broken before. They crunched under foot when I stepped in, making Parker whirl around to face me in a panic, wielding a knife.

"I told you to stay outside!" he barked, but his outburst barely registered in my mind. Whoever broke into Parker's place had trashed it good.

The couches and two bean bags were ripped, stuffing and springs poking out from the fabric. His computer and TV were smashed in, the bookshelves had been tossed to the ground, and his games and books littered the floor. The kitchen was pretty much the same, and I assumed his bedroom was a disaster zone too.

"Why would anyone do this?" I gasped, walking toward him. That was when I noticed the photo in Parker's other hand. The burglar had ripped it out of its frame. Parker rushed to hide it in his back pocket, but I snatched it up before he could. "Does this have anything to do with John Dobbs? Did he vandalize your home?" The photo in question was the one of Parker, John, and the girl whose name I still did not know. But now, Parker's face had been scratched out until there was just a hole where his face should have been.

"It was probably the punk kids who broke into my house last time. The cops never made an arrest. More like they never bothered to follow up on my report," he spat, running his fingers through his hair. He took a shuddering breath, taking in the mess, and then jerked as if he'd been electrocuted. "Di, we need to find Kibbles!"

My heart skipped a beat. The adorable little cat had completely escaped my mind. After hearing about that disgusting prank his former neighbors had played on Parker, I shuddered to think what those vile monsters would do to his pet. We split up when we didn't find Kibbles in or around the house and searched the cemetery. Kibbles liked to wander around, so she could have simply gone off to explore somewhere, but given what we had come home to...

Parker called for me just as a police cruiser pulled up at the gates. He had Kibbles cradled in his arms, one foot in the air as she cleaned herself. Sighing in relief, I jogged up to the house so that the two officers could take my statement as well.

Parker and I told them what happened. He also brought up the previous break-in case involving the high school kids, but he didn't once mention John Dobbs. I tried to mention it myself, but Parker cut me off with a glacial glare. Grinding my jaw out of frustration, I played with Kibbles and listened quietly as he told the cops that nothing had been taken despite the place being torn apart.

I didn't get why he didn't want the police knowing about

John. If he was the one behind this, the police could arrest him—problem solved. But no, Parker was determined to blame this on a group of teenagers who'd barely even been around the graveyard since we'd started dating. Besides, the fact that nothing was stolen screamed personal motive to me.

"We'll try to get our forensics team here as soon as possible, tomorrow afternoon at the latest. For now, I would suggest you not sleep here for the night. You don't want to destroy evidence or be in the line of fire if the person who did this decides to come back," one of the officers advised, snapping his notebook shut. The two officers said their goodbyes and walked back to the cruiser.

Parker kicked a pile of leaves that he'd raked around his house, clenching and unclenching his fists.

"You can stay at my place for the night. Greta won't mind," I offered, rubbing soothing circles into his back. He was wound up tighter than a coiled spring, his shoulders weighted down as if he was carrying the rest of the world with him.

Ignoring what the cops had said about not disturbing evidence, Parker packed a bag of clothes that hadn't met the business end of a knife and grabbed everything Kibbles would need for the night. With one last troubled look at his place, Parker locked it up and we drove to my house.

CHAPTER 14

It had been Greta's day off, so she'd been home when we showed up, meaning Parker and I couldn't exactly talk freely. The spare bedroom downstairs was filled with my art projects and a bunch of other stuff that Greta and I had nowhere else to keep, so Parker had trudged up to my room moments after we'd arrived and closeted himself up there while I explained to Greta what had happened. She then went to her Bible group while I decided to give Parker some space and went to the spare room to work on a painting that had been scratching at the back of my mind.

I was working on a painting for the gallery showing. Unlike other artists, my collections didn't have a specific theme. If you looked through the canvases in the room, you'd find landscape paintings of places around Mystic Cove or fantastical settings that I came up with. The one I was working on at the moment was one such fantasy piece, inspired by Parker. I supposed you could call it a fan art of sorts. In my mind, I'd dubbed it The Ice Prince. I'd only started working on it the previous day, and there wasn't much to make out except a pair of glacial white eyes with flecks of blue fiercely glaring at me. I had my air pods on, humming along to Panic! At The Disco's "Emperor's New Clothes," when the earpiece in my left ear was pulled out.

"Are those my eyes?" Parker asked over my shoulder. A sharp scream escaped me at the unexpected intrusion. Somehow, my stool tipped back, toppling me over, taking Parker down along with me. I lost grip of the acrylic paint palette in my hand and it smeared all over my baggy Metallica shirt. Beneath me, Parker groaned when I accidentally elbowed him in the kidneys as I struggled to get up off him.

"Dude, why'd you sneak up on me like that? Nearly gave me a friggin' heart attack!" I groaned, rubbing a hand over my racing heart. Parker sat up on the floor, massaging the spot where I'd hit him.

"I called your name a few times, but you didn't hear me because of this." He held up the earpiece he'd snatched from me.

I snatched my earpiece back. "Dude, that is so rude. I was in the zone."

"Sorry," he said, getting up and looking at the painting again. "My eyes really look like that to you? They look like crushed diamonds."

"Yeah," I said, my irritation at being interrupted wearing off. "Don't they look like that to you? I mean, you see them more than I do. Every time you look in the mirror."

He shrugged. "I don't look at myself too closely. I don't look like...me...anymore."

I nodded thoughtfully. "I guess you do look different from how you did when you were human. But you're still you, you know?"

He sighed. "I don't know. Maybe. Sometimes I—"

He got cut off as his phone buzzed. He glanced down and shut it off. I held my breath, waiting for him to pick up where he'd left off. He was finally opening up to me, but his stupid phone—

It buzzed again. He looked at it and started to shut it off, but my annoyance took over.

"Who is it?"

"Nothing," he said, but as soon as he put the phone back in his pocket, it started buzzing again.

"Maybe it's something important," I said through gritted teeth. "Answer it." Parker shook his head and was going to shut the call down again, but I reached for his phone and looked at the caller ID. "It's John."

"I know," Parker said, grabbing the phone back. "Why do you think I keep hanging up on him?"

The phone stopped ringing for a moment, only to start back up again.

"Answer the phone," I growled, tired of this middle-school nonsense.

"No," he said. He pulled the phone out to hang up on another ring, and I yanked the phone away again.

"Then I will," I said, tapping the green answer button. "Hell—"

"Don't!" The phone was snatched from my hand. Parker cut the call off and tossed the phone clear across the room. He looked back at me, his arms crossed, as if he was daring me to go find the phone and answer it when it started buzzing again.

"Real mature," I said. I shook my head as I left the room to go take a shower. I was still covered in paint from when he'd surprised me, and I didn't want to mess with him and his zombie clan drama. If he wasn't going to let me in and tell me what was going on, I wasn't going to get involved.

I didn't need this crap. No woman needs an emotionally absent guy. Especially one that wouldn't even be honest about what was going on in his life.

Some soulmate! I couldn't wait to tell Beverly that she'd finally failed. I turned the shower water on as hot as I could handle and climbed inside, vowing to let my troubles wash down the drain. If Parker was gone when I got back out, it was no skin off my nose.

***

Parker had his back to me when I entered the kitchen, staring out into the darkening street. Part of me was glad to still see him there. For a moment, it gave me hope that we could work things out. That he had come to his senses and was going to open up to me. But then I saw that on the counter next to him was a bottle of Bacardi white rum I'd stolen from Dad's office eons ago and a shot glass that was already drained off its contents.

"What are you still doing here? And did you just... Are you drinking that rum straight up?" I gaped at his back in shock. The Parker I knew was a light beer guy.

"Parker!" I barked when he refused to acknowledge my presence and poured himself another shot. Stalking up to the sink, I grabbed the glass from his hand, dumped the contents into the sink, and took the rum away as well. How dare he steal my booze!

"I was drinking that." His tone was dry and matter-of-fact, lethargic even. His eyes were glazed, but I don't think it was because he was already buzzed. He was in pain, but I was angry because I didn't know why he was hurting so I couldn't help him get through this. Because he wouldn't let me!

"I'm getting sick and tired of asking the same thing over and over again. I am not a broken record, so if you don't want to tell me what's going on, that's fine. Either by my boyfriend and talk to me or leave. I won't accept silence."

I cocked my hands on my hips, watching and waiting for a reaction, any reaction at all, but got nothing. A sharp pain sliced through my chest and my vision became blurry. I was not a crier; in fact, I was the type to laugh during emotional moments when watching a movie. In real life, I chose to drink my emotions away or bury them deep until I couldn't take it anymore. And then I would cry in bulk. It was like a spring cleaning of the soul, usually in the privacy of my bathroom where I could pretend my tears were just water droplets from the shower sluicing down my body. Not a healthy coping mechanism, I know, but I'd been doing it for so long, I didn't know any other way.

Parker and I stared at each other, at an impasse with his secret a gaping chasm between us. The sound of a car door banging somewhere down the street broke through the moment. I wiped away the tears pooling in my eyes with more force than necessary and hugged myself as a sense of hopelessness washed over me.

"Drink away your problems if you want, but I'm not going to stick around until you decide to pull your head out of your butt. I'll bring down some blankets and pillows. You can sleep on the couch tonight, but tomorrow you're on your own. You can go back to grandpa's dorm or whatever." More tears pooled in my eyes, my nose itching with the need to bawl my eyes out, but I wouldn't let myself make a noise until I was safely behind my bedroom door. But I meant what I said. I wasn't going to accept being given the silent treatment from a grown man. He could either talk to me and we could work things out, or he could leave.

"John thinks I killed his daughter!" Parker blurted, stopping me in my tracks.

CHAPTER 15

*P*arker's confession lingered in the air like a miasma, but I giggled uncontrollably. I turned to face him, a hand over my mouth to stifle my laughter, but I was unable to stop. Shadows crept across the kitchen floor, twisted and misshapen like wraiths coming to drag me away.

I bit down on my lip hard enough to draw blood, my breath coming in shallow gasps. I was waiting for Parker to break down laughing as well. I waited for him to make fun of my shell-shocked expression and mock me for believing what he'd said. It had to be a joke, right? Parker wasn't capable of killing someone. But I don't think he was even breathing. His pulse fluttered furiously at his neck, echoing mine.

"You killed someone?" Not just someone—his clan leader's daughter. There were so many implications to this revelation, and none of them computed in my brain because I was torn between this image Parker had planted in my mind of himself as a killer and this adorkable man I was falling in love with. Wasn't that a shot to the heart.

It wasn't like I was oblivious to my feelings for him; the

chemistry between us was undeniable and I cared for him a great deal. It's just that I thought that when I fell in love, there would be this big production around it, like that one moment when it would strike me like lightning. Like, Boom! You're in love! But it had snuck up on me. Fondness, admiration, adoration—an amalgamation of various emotions that mixed and melded together and before I knew it, I was in love. With a murderer, apparently.

I swayed on my feet, and Parker was there to catch me. What did it say about me that I immediately nuzzled into his touch and calmed down from having his crispy clean scent blanket me? How could I be comforted by a murderer?

The flecks of blue in Parker's eyes blazed, the only spot of color against his otherwise pale complexion and hair. He held on tight, as if afraid I would bolt the second he let me go. Or maybe it was to stop me from shivering like a leaf in the rain. His thumbs brushed across the blade of my cheekbone and he tilted my head so that I could no longer avoid his gaze.

"No. I said John thinks I killed his daughter. The whole clan does, but the evidence they have against me is circumstantial at best. The only reason I ran instead of staying to defend myself was because they were all willing to shoot first and ask questions later. I couldn't take that risk." Sincerity shimmered in his eyes. My eyebrows knit in confusion at his explanation. Parker took my hand and tugged me into the living room.

"Greta will be back soon. Maybe we should talk upstairs?" I led him up to my bedroom and settled down at the foot of my bed, watching him pick up his phone, set it down on the dressing table, and start pacing.

"You're making me dizzy," I grumbled, getting up and pulling him to sit next to me.

"I don't know where to start," Parker said, his voice a naked blade of emotion.

I laced our fingers together and brought his hand up to my lips. "The beginning is always a great place to start."

Parker poked his tongue in the side of his cheek as he looked up at the ceiling. He kept clenching and unclenching the hand that was holding mine. "So, I told you that after my parents and I had a falling out, John took me in. There is a small neighborhood in Bloomington, where I lived, that is made up of zombies only. Like a tiny village of extended relatives, or so John used to describe it. Everyone had normal jobs and we mingled with the rest of the city, but in that neighborhood, we never had to shy away from who we were. John took me in, let me live under his roof, and taught me what it meant to be a zombie. That's where I met and fell in love with Layla."

Parker's confession caught me off guard. I visibly flinched at his admission that he was—still was?—in love with someone else. Layla had to be the girl in the photo back at his house. She was dead, killed, but that didn't mean Parker didn't love her anymore. Was I competing with a ghost? A cheap replacement for what he lost? Ugh, I wasn't thinking rationally! How could I be jealous of a dead woman?

"What—" My voice cracked. I cleared my throat before asking, "What happened to her, to Layla?"

Parker chuckled. His laugh was low and deep. I felt it move through me, leaving goosebumps pebbled on my skin.

"What is it?"

Parker shifted, closing the space between us on the couch. In an impressive display of strength, he lifted me up and took my spot, settling me down sideways on his lap. "I just think that you're cute when you're jealous." He nuzzled into me and placed a chaste kiss on my lips. Scowling at him,

I poked his cheek and demanded he get on with the story. His arms banded around my midsection. I had no idea what to do with my hands, so I started drawing random patterns along the length of his arms.

"I was not in a good place mentally and emotionally after my transition. It was stressful enough being a human teenage boy going through puberty. Imagine transitioning into a creature you thought was fictional. Add in abandonment and anger issues, and I was a basket case and a real jerk to be around. All John wanted was to help me adjust, but for that first year or so, I wouldn't let him."

Somehow, I struggled with imagining Parker as a jackass. Okay, I take that back. He was one just a moment ago, but even then, that was because he was under extreme emotional distress. Which I supposed he would have been under so soon after his transition and having his family turn their backs on him.

"And that's where Layla came in. She was older than me by three years, so she was twenty-one when we met. A real spitfire." His lips wobbled, eyes going bright with the sheen of unshed tears, but he didn't break down. Clearing his throat and wiping away the tears, he gave me a bashful smile and continued with his tale. "She was just like me. When she was sixteen, Layla and her family were attacked by a rabid clan of zombies and everyone but her was slain. Like me, John took her in and eased her into her second life as a zombie. So, while I was a bit resistant to trust that John was only trying to help me, it was easier to let Layla in through the walls I'd built around myself."

"She sounds like just what you needed," I said. I was trying to sound magnanimous. I meant the words. Parker was alone and terrified. He needed someone to help him, someone he could trust and confide in, and Layla sounded like just that. But I guess the words didn't sound the way I meant them to.

"Hey, look at me," Parker ordered in that gentle, yet firm way of his, cupping my face with both of his hands. The way he said it, I had no choice but to obey. My heart skipped a beat and my breath stalled in my lungs from the depth of emotion swimming in his pale eyes. Not just any emotion— the emotion. The one that poets, singers, and writers had spent centuries trying to encapsulate in words.

"I don't want you to think I'm still hung up on Layla. I won't lie and say that I'm over losing her, but I have moved on with my life. What I feel for you... I love you, Dianna Flowers. more than I ever thought possible. That's why I'm still here with you. You don't know how tempted I was to just pack up my stuff and leave once I realized that John had found me, but I couldn't stand the idea of losing you." He looked like he still had more to say, but I shut him up with a kiss, curling my fingers in his hair and straddling him, stopping only when our bodies screamed out for oxygen.

"Tell me the rest," I murmured against his lips, smirking at his kicked puppy look when I didn't give him the words he wanted to hear. All in due time. For now, I needed to know what we were dealing with. John Dobbs was practically stalking him, and if he was the one behind the break-in, he was escalating, and we needed to stop him before he hurt Parker.

"Layla was like an older sibling figure to me at first. She and John filled in the void left behind by my family. But my and Layla's relationship soon progressed into a more romantic one. But she was dating someone else at the time, so I was content to remain as her best friend/younger brother. But when I was twenty-three, four years ago, she broke things off with her boyfriend, Devin. The guy was the worst. He was loaded and came from a prominent witch family, so he was majorly enti-tled. He didn't like it much when Layla froze him out and decided she'd give us a chance. It was a whole mess. There was a point when I had to step in and force the guy to back off. I thought it had worked. For four months, we neither saw nor heard from him. We were happy, or at least I was happy."

Oh-oh. I had to consciously relax my muscles when I heard Parker's foreboding words. I wanted to see his face better, so I moved off his lap and sat cross-legged on the bed, my body angled toward him. We didn't bother switching on the lights beforehand, so the only light coming in was through the windows. From the bathroom, I could make out the drip, drip, drip of the faucet. The repetitive sound was driving me nuts, but I didn't want to disturb Parker by getting up to tighten the tap.

"Was Layla not happy?" I prodded when it looked like he was getting too lost in his memories. Eyebrows furrowed in consternation, Parker shrugged.

"That's just the thing, I never got the chance to find out. I was enrolled in college, studying computer programming and multimedia design."

"Because you wanted to be a videogame developer," I guessed, and Parker hummed in confirmation.

"Layla and I managed to snag ourselves a one-bedroom apartment near the university and everything. One day, I forgot an assignment and had to rush back to the apartment and found her and Devin in bed together," he explained, his fingers tensing around his knees. The only comfort I could give him was to curl my hand around his arm and cuddle into his side. I'd never been cheated on, so I couldn't imagine what must have gone through Parker's mind at the time.

"She claimed it was a one-off mistake, but I was too hurt to listen to anything she had to say and stormed out. My solution was to get drunk, but that's where things get hazy.

The bar I went to was owned by one of our clan members and was often frequented by the clan and zombies from other clans and other supernaturals. According to Cooper—Layla's best friend—Layla found me there and tried to drag me home, but I went off on her, going as far as to shove her away from me. I woke up the next day on a friend's couch with John's hands around my neck. He was screaming, accusing me of killing Layla. But I don't remember a thing that happened after I went to the bar."

"I don't understand. John and everyone else assume that you killed Layla just because you were seen fighting in a bar the night of the murder? What about the ex? Maybe he was jealous that Layla went after you. What if she told him the same thing she told you—that sleeping with him was a mistake and she still wanted to be with you? Sounds like a motive to me." I got up and started pacing the living room. "Wasn't there any forensic evidence?"

Parker scrubbed a hand down his face and regarded me from beneath his lashes. "He had a solid alibi for where he was at Layla's estimated time of death."

"And you have none," I surmised, my heart sinking. "Is there any proof? Not that I believe you did it," I rushed to add. "I just want to understand why John believes so whole-heartedly that you were the one that killed her when you clearly loved her so much. He's been on your tail for the past four years because of it."

"The 'evidence'—" He crooked his fingers to make air quotes and rolled his eyes. "—is circumstantial at best. One of my gym shirts, which I wasn't even wearing at the time, was found stashed in the bathroom trash bin covered in blood, and there was blood on the soles of my sneakers, which were also found in the bathroom for anyone to find. The knife..." His voice trembled and he had to take a moment to gather himself. He pulled his bottom lip between his teeth and his eyes squinted as he went through the list of supposed evidence. A frantic voice message from Layla to Parker, begging for forgiveness and asking him to come home. The fact that he was seen leaving the bar fifteen minutes before Layla's determined time of death. And their friend, Cooper, the one whose couch Parker ended up crashing on, testified that Parker only showed up at his front door two hours after he left the bar. More than enough time for Parker to head over to his and Layla's apartment, kill her, and drunkenly stumble his way to Cooper's place.

"What about DNA? Did Layla fight back? Were there any defensive wounds or skin under her fingernails? Anything conclusive to pin the murder on you? I'm guessing not since you've never been arrested."

Despite the rather morbid topic of discussion, Parker flashed me an amused smile, but it was gone just as quickly. "You listen to way too many murder podcasts, babe. I don't know if there was any DNA evidence, but I don't remember having any bruising or scratches the day after. But then again, I was preoccupied with stopping John from ripping my head off my neck. Zombie clans operate much like shifter packs. They would have executed me for Layla's murder without hesitation."

My heart kicked against my ribs and images of Parker's lifeless body flashed behind my closed lids.

"For what it's worth, I believe you," I told Parker. "I don't think you killed her, whether you were drunk or not, and we will find a way to prove that you didn't."

Parker gave me a grateful smile, but there was no hope in his eyes on the possibility of clearing his name. "That's easier said than done, Petal. How do we find evidence to exonerate me of a murder that happened four years ago?"

"Easy. We consult a witch." I beamed, an idea taking shape in my mind.

CHAPTER 16

Monday morning dawned bright and early. Parker and I were already having a shushed argument in the kitchen when I heard Greta turn on the shower upstairs.

"You're being unreasonable. I thought you wanted to get John off your back!" I hissed through my teeth, slamming a steaming cup of coffee on the counter in front of him. The dark liquid sloshed over the rim and splashed onto the counter, almost splattering on Parker's lavender shirt—one of his few work shirts that hadn't gotten ripped to shreds.

He gave me a narrow-eyed glare and reached for a cloth to wipe the counter. "Call me crazy, but putting the word out there that I am a wanted fugitive on suspicion of murder doesn't sound much like aiding our cause. If anything, I think it'll give the naysayers a valid excuse to bring out the torches and pitchforks," he snarked, walking around me to rinse the cloth as I dished out waffles and bacon for the both of us and poured myself a glass of orange juice. I rolled my eyes. Parker was overreacting and he knew it. My plan was the best shot he had at clearing his name without having to return to his former clan and actively re-investigate the case.

"I never said we should blast this from the town hall's speakers. I simply suggested we consult Beverley, who you very well know would never betray your confidence. She has a bevy of spells and enchantments at her disposal, some of which could unlock your memories—"

A loud thud came from upstairs, followed by Greta cursing. I stopped to listen to see if she was coming downstairs. Vampires had excellent hearing, though, so even though Parker and I were already having a whispered argument, I lowered my voice even further.

"All I'm saying is we should ask Bev if she can unlock your lost memories from that night with John present to watch. If Bev does that and casts a spell to prevent you from telling lies, then John will have solid proof that you never hurt his daughter," I insisted.

"And what makes you think John won't kill me on sight? I'm not calling him, Di, and we're not telling Beverley, okay? Am I making myself clear?"

I growled in frustration, curling my hands in the air and imagining that I was strangling his pencil neck.

"Why are you being so stubborn about this? Do you intend to live your whole life on the run? If so, what does that mean for us because I didn't sign up for this!" I regretted the word the moment they were out of my lips. A tsunami-sized wave of remorse crushed me when Parker visibly flinched from the impact of my words.

He stared blankly into his coffee and pushed off his seat to dump the contents into the sink. "I'm scared. Terrified of what we'll find when we start rooting through my head. All these years, I've convinced myself that I was innocent, that there was no way I was capable of murder, no way I could kill Layla. But somewhere in the deepest, darkest recesses of my heart and mind...I've always wondered. I have a whole chunk of memories missing. Is it simply because I was drunk? I only remember having two beers with Cooper, but he claims I was totally plastered. Or is my subconscious blocking off an extremely traumatic event to keep my mind from splintering apart?"

Parker held onto the rim of the kitchen sink as if it were the only thing holding him together, his fingers and knuckles turning white from the strength of his grip. His face was turned away from me so that I couldn't see the expression, but I imagined it was as shattered as my heart felt.

"What if... What if I—"

I stood behind him and wrapped my hands around his midsection, laying my cheek against his back. "You didn't do it, Parker. I'm sure of it."

"How can you be so sure?" he croaked, making no move to embrace me or push me away. In that moment, he sounded very much like a lost child and felt like fragile glass in my arms. He was like a sandcastle bracing itself against an oncoming wave that knows its attempt to hold its ground is futile. In the end, it would be swept away regardless of its determination. But Parker was no sandcastle. He was mine, and I refused to let him give up on himself—on us—without fighting back.

"I just do. No more running, Parker. We're going to figure this out because I plan on keeping you around for a long, long time. And since I happen to be extremely fond of Mystic Cove, this is where I want the two of us to build our life. Together." It wasn't the three magic words he'd said to me last night in my bedroom, but it was the closest to a confession of love I had ever admitted to.

Because I had my cheek against Parker's back, I caught

the flutter of his heart and felt his muscles move and shift beneath my fingers.

"Ditto, Petal," he replied.

When he heard the thud of Greta's footsteps on the stairs, we tabled the discussion for later, but come what may, I would find a way to convince Parker that this was our best shot. In the meantime, I planned to locate John Dobbs on my own.

***

Turned out, I didn't need to put much effort into scouring the town for John. A shame since I was looking forward to getting my Sherlock on.

In fact, John Dobbs found me.

I didn't recognize him at first as I waited in line for my and Beverley's usual morning order at Jumpin' Beans. In a cheap imitation of every Marvel character ever, he wore a baseball cap to cover his pale blonde hair and to obscure his face, and he stood two people behind me in line. He waited until I'd received my order and then stepped out of the line to approach me.

"Dianna Flowers?" His voice was hoarse and gravelly, as if his throat had been crushed at some point in the past. Gooseflesh broke out across my body and the hairs on my arms stood on end. Not human, definitely not human my instincts screamed at me. The only reason I didn't listen to them was because we were in a crowded coffee shop filled with vampires, shifters, witches, and even the sheriff—human—was having his breakfast as he scowled at a document in his free hand.

"Who's asking?" I arched my eyebrow, injecting as much bravado and attitude in my tone as I could muster.

The corners of his lips quirked up in a barely there smile at my posturing and he took off his sunglasses and cap, showing off his pale, blue eyes. A zombie.

"John," I stated calmly, the shock I was feeling in that moment not reflecting in my voice or demeanor.

"So, you know who I am." He seemed pleased by that fact. John was a tall man, way over the six-foot mark, and had the bearing of a soldier. Except for the stress lines bracketing the sides of his mouth and crow's feet fanning out from the corners of his eyes, his face was unlined. But I knew he had to be at least older than my dad—maybe even my grandfather.

"I do, and if you think you can use me to get to Parker, you should know I am no shrinking violet. I will take you down with me if I have to before I let you lay a hand on him. I sympathize with your loss, Mr. Dobbs, but Parker is not the one you're looking for, so save yourself the heartache and energy and go back to wherever the hell you came from," I bit out, getting a little hot under the collar. Belatedly I realized that even though the coffee shop was moderately noisy, at least half of the people present could hear what John and I were saying. He must have realized it too because he cast uneasy glances around the store, his face crinkling in consternation.

"I know that Parker was not behind Layla's murder—"

"Yeah, that's right—" I scoffed, cutting him off, ready to chew him up one side and down the other for ever suspecting that Parker could be responsible for such a thing when his words registered. "Come again?"

John winced as if it pained him to repeat himself. "I said that I know it wasn't Parker's fault. He didn't kill...Layla." He stumbled on Layla's name, an ancient pain darkening his pale eyes. Parker told me that Layla was not John's biological daughter, but that didn't make the pain of losing her any less keen.

"You know? For a fact? As in, you have concrete proof that Parker has been telling the truth this whole time?"

"Yes!" John growled, growing impatient with me. "Can we please take this conversation somewhere private? I'm hoping that after you hear everything I have to say, you'll help me convince Parker to see me. Not only do I owe him an apology, but I have every reason to believe that he's in danger."

CHAPTER 17

PARKER

Today was not my day. Letting out a weary sigh, I minimized the document I was working on and tossed my glasses on the heap of files littering my desk. I reached for my phone, ready to call Dianna and tell her I'd changed my mind. Her idea was solid. If Beverley could somehow unearth my lost memories, then this dark cloud hanging over me would disappear and Layla could finally rest in peace. John would also get some closure. Some, because I didn't think the man would ever rest until Layla's true killer was brought to justice.

But what if you really are the killer? a smooth voice crooned in the back of my mind, a voice I'd learned to drown out over the last four years. I'd convinced myself that I couldn't have been the one to kill Layla, no matter how hurt or angry I was about her betrayal. I was not a violent person. But that niggling doubt had been with me constantly, burrowing and working its way deep into my psyche, eating away at me and making me question if I was a monster after all. What would I do if the truth Beverley unearthed was not the one I wanted—no, needed to hear?

143

Was it worth it to risk losing everything? Dianna? My newfound home? Everything for answers I wasn't sure I wanted to hear?

As if I didn't have enough to worry about, the police had gone through my house once again. I wished I could say I trusted that they would find evidence that it was those high school punks who'd trashed my place. But even though I'd denied it to her face, Dianna likely had the right of it. I just hoped that John was smart enough not to leave any trace of himself behind. He was an ex-military man, meaning his prints and DNA were in the government database, easy for the cops to trace. If the local police learned why John was really in town, it was curtains for me. All those people who wanted me gone would have a justifiable reason to get rid of me. None of them would even consider the idea that I might be innocent.

A cool, comforting breeze trailed its fingers down my cheeks before skittering away. I huffed out a short laugh, wondering which of the people currently lying in the refrigerated drawers had invited themselves into my thoughts. You know you're a pathetic loser and coward when a ghost tries to comfort you.

What to do? What to do? Groaning, I dug the heel of my palms into my eyes and thumped my head down on the desk, lightly smashing my head on the computer's keyboard.

"Parker?" Mrs. Graham's voice called out in a trembling whisper, thick with tears. I sat up, spinning my chair to face the entrance to my lab, wondering why I didn't hear her come down the stairs.

"What's wrong?" I blurted out, jumping from my chair and struggling to comprehend what I was seeing. Mrs. Graham was pale as a ghost with silent tears trekking down her face and her hands held up in surrender. She was being held with an arm around her neck and a gun pressed to the side of her head. And her captor...

"Cooper?"

Seeing him again was like stepping years into the past. Except that this wasn't the same Cooper I'd left behind. He'd grown out his blond hair, more golden than your average zombie, and it cascaded down his back in greasy strings. He was gaunt. His cheeks and eyes were sunken in, and I could smell the stale scent of beer and cigarettes wafting off of him even though he was standing nine feet away.

"What's going on?" I took a step in his direction, but he growled out a warning to stay where I was, pressing the gun harder into Mrs. Graham's temple. She let out a whimper, her eyes silently pleading with me for help.

I could feel my heart pounding in my throat. The taste of blood coated my tongue—metallic and bitter. There was only one reason he could be here. The same reason John was after me. To get revenge for Layla's murder. Cooper and Layla were best friends, and when I came along, they effortlessly welcomed me into the fold even though I was younger and carried a boulder-sized chip on my shoulder, always acting out and behaving like an incorrigible brat.

When I decided to flee and stay under the radar, I never gave a single thought to how Cooper was dealing with the aftermath. He'd not only lost Layla, but he'd believed that it was his only other friend who'd killed her. As much as our clan liked to think of itself as a huge family, the fact of the matter was that Cooper only had Layla, John, and me in his life. Layla and John were the social glue that kept us connected to the rest of the clan, but Cooper was an even bigger loner than I was. In some ways, he reminded me of Emil, only stepping out of the safety of his home if either Layla or I were with him. He had a job as a tech consultant that allowed him to work from home. Looking at him now, he was a pale shadow of the man he used to be. Losing Layla broke something in him.

"I finally found you. Your time of reckoning has finally arrived and I will enjoy making you pay for taking her from me." Cooper bared his teeth in a cruel, twisted, predatory smile that sent chills skittering down my back.

"Please, please, let me go," Mrs. Graham whimpered, trying unsuccessfully to dislodge the arm Cooper had wrapped around her neck.

"Shut up! Unless you want to bite the bullet right now," Cooper barked, his finger hooked around the trigger.

"No!" I started to run toward them but stopped short when he turned the gun at me. I had enhanced healing, but not even that would help me against a fatal injury like a bullet between my eyes or a direct hit to the heart. Raising my hands, I took a couple more cautious steps, Cooper tracking my movement until there was at least a foot of distance between us.

"Coop, I know you blame me for what happened to Layla, but my boss has nothing to do with this. Let her go and we can talk about this, hmm?"

"It's your fault she's dead. Now John wants to welcome you back into the clan like you did nothing wrong? If you had never came into the picture, she would still be alive right now!" he screamed. An odd sort of horror settled over me once I processed his rant. I was a nervous wreck on the inside, screaming my head off, but somehow, I managed to keep my composure.

I dared not look away from Cooper's crazed eyes, but my brain worked furiously to find a way to get us all out of this unharmed. "What do you mean John wants to welcome me back? He thinks I killed Layla, same as you. But I didn't, I swear to God. I would never harm a hair on her head!"

Shock flashed through Cooper's eyes. For a short

moment, he lowered his gun, but he had it aimed back at Mrs. Graham before I could move and try to tackle him.

"So, you don't know... You still don't remember. Then what evidence was John talking about?" he murmured to himself.

My phone started to ring from where I'd left it on the desk, the vibrations echoing throughout the room and startling Cooper from his internal musings. He removed his hand from around Mrs. Graham's neck and threaded his fingers into her hair instead, tugging roughly at the strands until she had no choice but to bare her neck and stare up at the ceiling. The gun was aimed at me once again, and Cooper roughly pushed Mrs. Graham into the room and forced me to walk backward.

"What are you talking about? What don't I remember? Did you finally find the real killer?" Was that why John was seeking me out? To tell me that he knew I was innocent? To apologize?

Cooper chortled, his sneer injecting ice into my veins. There was something seriously wrong with him. I mean, him holding us hostage and pointing a gun at Mrs. Graham's head was an obvious clue. But this was more than grief-driven despair. Cooper wasn't all there, and something told me there would be no reasoning with him. The ringing on my phone ended, but picked up again a second later, somehow adding to the tension stifling the air in the room.

"I guess I should be glad that you've been suffering all this time, not knowing whether you killed your girlfriend or not. When I saw you with that goth chick, you have no idea what it took to stop me from killing her. How dare you be happy? How dare you move on with someone else after what you made me do? How dare you bask in the sun while her ghost torments me day and night and refuses to let me get any peace?" Cooper roared, glaring at a point over my shoulder.

If it were a normal human speaking, I would have disregarded that ghost comment, but given that zombies could actually interact with those on the other side of the veil... I whirled around, thinking there would be someone actually standing behind me. That I might actually see Layla again.

Nothing. Although... A familiar scent teased my senses. Vanilla, strawberries, and sunshine. Layla. Was she there? My eyes searched the room, looking for something, anything to indicate that she was there. I'd always wondered if she was resting in peace or if her spirit still lingered on this plane, hoping her murderer would be apprehended.

"Do you see her too, Parker? She won't let me have any peace. She hates me. She wants to kill me, but it's not my fault. You're the ones who made me do it." Cooper started crying, which triggered Mrs. Graham to start bawling too. I was frozen on the spot, my mind working to put the puzzle pieces together, and the picture they painted made bile rise in my throat.

"You didn't..." My voice was a ragged whisper.

"I had no choice!" Cooper roared. "She wouldn't see me, refused to see me. First, she bent herself backward and twisted herself in knots like a pretzel, trying to be good enough for that elitist warlock who didn't even deserve to lick the ground she walked on. When she finally saw how unworthy he was, I thought that maybe, just maybe..." He took a shuddering breath that shook his entire frame. "But then she looks at you like the sun rose and set in your eyes. I had to stand there like a moron, listening to her agonize over you two idiots. There's only so much a man can take." His voice cracked.

"Y-you killed her? You k-killed Layla," I stuttered. My legs threatened to give out from under me, so I gripped the edge of the autopsy table before they buckled. "Because you were jealous?" Incredulity colored my tone.

"It should have been me! I was there for all the highs and lows. I was the one she chose to confide in all the time. She called me her soulmate. So why? Why did she choose to debase herself with you and the warlock when I would have loved her as she deserved?" Cooper moaned like a dying animal. In the back of my mind, I did recall Layla saying something about Cooper being her best friend, her platonic soulmate. I guessed he had selective hearing and chose instead to focus on the soulmate part.

As if angered by this fact, the scent of Layla's perfume grew stronger, but the sweet aroma had changed and carried with it a note of decay and rot. Static electricity filled the room, raising the hairs on my arms and causing everything that wasn't nailed down in the room to start shaking. It was gentle at first, a vibrating hum that grew in intensity until it felt like we were stuck in the middle of an earthquake.

While Cooper was distracted by the commotion, Mrs. Graham managed to dislodge him by hooking her leg around his and forcibly tugging her hair from his grasp and elbowing him in the ribs.

"Go get help!" I yelled when she hesitated, probably wanting to take me with her, but Cooper was already rising to his feet. Mrs. Graham rushed up the stairs, but she wasn't going to make it. Cooper was already aiming his gun at her. I let out a battle roar and rushed him, taking the both of us to the ground. We rolled around on the floor until I pinned Cooper facedown underneath me and twisted his wrist until he dropped the gun and I pushed it away. He managed to buck me off him, the two of us quickly getting back on our feet and breaking into a brawl of fists and kicks as I tried to keep him from reaching for the gun.

"Parker!" Dianna rushed into the room, her blonde hair flying and eyes glassy with fear. My shock at seeing her cost me dearly. Cooper kicked out at my knees and rushed for the gun when I toppled to the ground. I had no time to call out a warning. It all happened so quickly, and yet every detail was crystal clear in my mind. The way Dianna's gaze widened just a fraction as her attention swung from me to Cooper and the mortal fear that darkened her olive eyes. John was screaming behind her, but it was too late to push her out of the way. The victorious shark-like smile on Cooper's face twisted as he squeezed the trigger. But none of that compared to the loud explosion imprinted into my mind when the gun went off or the way Dianna's face screwed up in pain right before she crumpled on the stairs and rolled down them.

Everything after that was a blur. I don't remember how I managed to grab the gun from Cooper. Later, I was told that I'd emptied the barrel into his chest. None of that mattered, not when the love of my life lay bleeding out a few feet away from me.

CHAPTER 18

My body was on fire, and I was lying on the world's most uncomfortable bed. There was an annoying beeping sound coming from somewhere. I wanted to tell whoever was responsible for it to turn it off, but my lips felt like they were sewn shut. My eyes too.

I thought I heard my mother crying and Dad's deep voice. I wanted to call out to them, but a thick warm fog wrapped around me like a down blanket. The next time I rose to consciousness, it was to a cool hand brushing hair away from my forehead. I managed to open my eyes, despite my lids weighing a ton, and immediately screwed them shut from the blinding overhead lights.

"The lights..." I groaned, or at least that's what I thought I said. My body and my brain were not in sync.

"Di? Sweetheart, can you hear me?" Parker's hands on my face were like a soothing balm against the uncomfortable heat writhing all over my body. He was saying something, but I was too preoccupied with trying to figure out what was going on. I guessed I was in the hospital; it was the only place that smelled like antiseptic and misery. That beeping had to be from a monitor. I could spy an IV drip from the corner of my eyes when they fluttered open once again.

Like a dam bursting under pressure, memories of how I ended up in the hospital bed came flooding to me. I'd been shot. It was Cooper, the third person in the photograph. After John asked to talk privately, I led him to The Book Coven, where he told me—and Beverley, because I wasn't dumb enough to be alone with him without backup—about what really happened.

It was all a little hazy, but I remembered John saying something about Cooper having psychotic episodes. He'd recently confessed to killing Layla in a fit of rage. When the realization of what he'd done settled in, he'd set up Parker to take the fall by drugging him so that he wouldn't remember what happened the night before.

Cooper went missing after he told John the truth. John had given him twenty-hour hours to go to the cops and turn himself in. Instead, Devin, the warlock Layla had dated, turned up dead, murdered, and Copper had fled. So John had upped his search for Parker, fearing that he would be the next target.

Upon hearing all that, I'd tried to call Parker and grew panicked when his phone went to voicemail three times. We'd then rushed to the funeral home and bumped into Mrs. Graham, crying and screaming for help. Without waiting to hear what had happened, I'd rushed down to Parker's lab and next thing I knew there was a bullet in my gut.

"Babe?" Parker called out again. Gasping, I pushed myself up, needing to see that he was unharmed with my own eyes. The sudden movement aggravated my injuries, leaving me breathless, and I slumped back on the bed.

"Take it easy, you don't want to pull your stitches. Should I call the doctor?" he asked, already getting up and making his way toward the door.

"Wait!" I croaked. Parker paused at the doorway and walked back to me. He helped prop me up and adjusted the pillow behind my back. His smile shook like he was fighting to keep it on and not break down in tears. I reached for his hand, noting that he was not in a hospital gown and that there wasn't a single scratch on him.

"Cooper... Did he hurt you?" I breathed through the pulsating pain in my gut.

Parker gaped incredulously. "Me? Babe, you got shot in the stomach. The doctor said you were lucky that the bullet missed your liver, but they still had to go in and remove it, as well as stop the internal bleeding. I could have lost you. I could have—" A hiccup wrecked through his body, a single tear dropping down onto our joined hands. "Don't ever do that to me again."

I tugged him toward me and hugged him even though my stitches protested. Parker buried his face in the crook of my neck, breathing in my scent. I cringed inwardly, realizing that I probably stank. Running my fingers through his unruly hair, I murmured softly, assuring him that I was fine and wasn't going anywhere. When he finally stopped trembling, I asked him what had happened to Cooper.

"I killed him." His confession was a broken, haunted whisper. "After I saw you...like that, I grabbed the gun and emptied it into his chest. I made sure he couldn't heal from that." He peered up at me as if waiting for me to reject him.

"Good," I stated plainly, brushing his hair away from his forehead. His eyes looked especially large thanks to the magnifying effect of his glasses. It was almost comical. His forehead crinkled, his jaw dropping open at my declaration.

"I tell you I killed a man and all you have to say is 'good'?"

"You tell me that you killed the man who killed your ex-girlfriend and her former lover, a man who wanted to kill you and shot me. So, yeah, good. You were only defending yourself and everyone else...unless... Do the cops say different?"

Parker shook his head and grabbed the cup of water by my bedside when my voice cracked and I started coughing. He waited for me to finish drinking before explaining.

"John stepped in and told them everything. Given what happened, the sheriff was inclined to file the shooting under self-defense."

"So, you finally talked to John, huh? How did that go down?" I asked.

Parker sighed and started playing with my fingers. "It was...intense. Basically, he told me how he discovered that it was Cooper all along, apologized for blaming for all these years, and told me I had a home waiting for me in the clan if I wanted to go back."

"And do you?" I pushed down the stab of panic, although the heart monitor betrayed me.

Parker smiled, his eyes lighting up for the first time since I'd woken up. "You are my home now. Where you go, I go—forever and always."

Something settled inside me after hearing his answer. We talked some more, until the nurse came to check in on me and gave me my next dose of painkillers when the dull throb of my wound turned into a raging inferno. I fell asleep to the sound of Parker's voice as he read Stephen King to me. I woke up the next day to find my parents in my room. Mom blubbered throughout the entire visit, fluffing my pillows, arranging and rearranging flowers.

When she stepped out to use the bathroom, an awkward-ness settled in when Dad and I were left alone. I waited for him to lay into me for everything that had happened. To harp on about how right he was about Parker and ask, *Why do you always make the wrong choices, Dianna Flowers?*

But none of those things passed through his lips. Instead,

he hugged me close and fervently apologized for all the crap we'd been fighting about. Turned out, he'd already cleared the air with Parker while I was unconscious. That day, my hospital room was a revolving door of visitors as all my friends, siblings, and even Beverley came to check in on me.

EPILOGUE

month and a half later, I watched from a distance as Parker talked to Layla and placed her favorite flowers at the base of her tombstone. He'd wanted me to join him, but I thought they deserved some privacy, so I wandered the cemetery instead.

It was my idea to travel to Minnesota so that Parker could finally lay her memory to rest after he told me that he sensed her presence in the mortuary the day I'd been shot. I shuddered, remembering the way it felt when the bullet pierced my stomach and thought I felt a phantom pain where the wound had scarred over. Parker had also decided that he wanted to reconnect with John. We'd spent the entire weekend at his place, and now that I knew he wasn't trying to kill my boyfriend, I rather liked John. Parker had left it until the day we were scheduled to head back to Mystic Cove to visit Layla's grave.

His family was in the area too, but whenever I brought up visiting them, Parker changed the subject. I let him bury the issue for now. I was sure that this wouldn't be the last time we would be visiting Minnesota, but some wounds take longer to heal than others. For now, it was enough that he had taken the first step by returning to this place that had caused him so much heartache.

I was reading the epitaph on a tombstone that had me snickering—*Wiley Jefferson, he loved his bacon*—when I heard a branch snap behind me.

"I feel like that could apply to you too," Parker said, gathering my hair and pulling it over my shoulder to kiss the back of my neck. A delicious shiver worked its way down my body.

I laid my head back on his chest and looked up through the tree limbs to the cool sun peeking through. I took in a deep breath and closed my eyes. I would never understand why some people found graveyards to be creepy. To me, they were the most peaceful place imaginable.

"Thank you for pushing me to come back here, and for coming with me," Parker said into the silence. A lazy breeze picked up and swirled around us, carrying the scent of vanilla and strawberries. It was like getting kissed by the wind. I was sure it was Layla, giving us her blessing.

"Wherever you go, I follow. I love you, Parker Smith."

"Ditto, Petal. Now, let's get you home. You have an exhibit to prepare for." After I was discharged from the hospital, Mr. Grayson and I finally decided on a date for the exhibit. It was this coming Friday and I still had a hundred and one things to do, all of which seemed a hundred times more difficult with the pains in my stomach I was still dealing with. But I had no end of extra hands to help me. Parker, my parents, my siblings. Weird how a near-death experience can bring you so much closer to the people you love.

Hand in hand, Parker and I walked toward the exit, and

that's when I decided to bring up something that had been on my mind all weekend. "I was going to wait for you to tell me the news, but we've been here all week and you've not said a word, so I'll just tell you now. I already know that you turned down Mrs. Graham's offer to take over the funeral home and that you re-enrolled in college to complete your degree."

Parker tripped over his feet, looking in my direction so fast that I feared he'd get whiplash. "You knew? How?"

"You left your laptop open to the university's homepage. Why were you all so cloak and dagger about it? Did you think I would try and stop you?"

"Yes. No. Both? I was going to tell you, but I wanted to wait and see if I could make it into the program first. I'm keeping the job at the funeral home for now; I'll need to pay my tuition bills somehow. And I'll be taking the courses online, so I'll still be around."

"Even if you had to move to the city, it would change nothing between us. You can't get rid of me that easily. I'm like a worm; I got my hooks deep into you."

Parker let out a groan, his face screwed in disgust. "Thank you for putting that image in my head. How am I supposed to kiss you now?"

"Easy, just like this." I grabbed the lapels of his denim jacket and pulled him toward me. Thankfully, I'd worn heeled boots, so I didn't have to get on my tiptoes to kiss him. I still needed to work on rebuilding my core. Parker gave in almost immediately, opening his mouth when I flicked my tongue along his lips. All the blood rushed to my head and a breathy moan escaped me when he licked at me like I was a delicious plate of cream. I cursed when he pulled away way too soon, leaving me weak in the knees with my clothes feeling rough against my goose-pimply skin.

"What's wrong?" I asked.

"Nothing," he said. "I just don't want to hurt you. You're still healing."

I sighed. He was right. But at this point in our relationship, my injury was the only thing keeping us from ripping each other's clothes off.

"Absence makes the heart grow fonder, right?" I said with a shrug.

"It will be worth the wait, I'm sure," he said, tapping my nose as we walked toward the rental car.

"You really don't mind that I want to go back to school?" he asked me again on the drive to the airport.

"For the last time, I'm not mad, and I don't mind that you want to get your degree and finally start working in a field you love. In fact, with me by your side, we'll take the gaming world by storm."

Parker's laughter filled up the car, lighting up everything within me.

"So..." I started, hesitating to ask the question that had been on my mind for weeks. "Are we mates now, like in the shifter sense?" From what I'd heard, the mating bond between shifters and vampires was a... Well, it wasn't an actual, tangible, physical tether, but you could feel it inside you. You could sense your partner within you and sometimes experience their emotions. But it wasn't like that with Parker and me. There wasn't, like, another presence in my head, but I knew for sure that he was it for me. There was no getting bored of him after a couple of months. He was my forever.

Beverly could add one more notch to her belt, I was sure.

"I don't think zombies have a mating bond the same as shifters, but yeah, you're my mate and I am yours. We're stuck with each other." He took my hand and raised it to his lips while he kept his gaze on the road.

"Like warts," I quipped, making him laugh again. It was

my favorite sound in the world, and I planned on hearing it
for the rest of my days.

THE END

AFTERWORD

I hope you enjoyed reading *My Blind Date is a Zombie*! If you did, please consider joining my mailing list so you never miss a new release!
DaphneBloom.com

books2read.com/gardenofhope

Can two lost causes find love in the arms of one another?

Lily, the peculiar youngest daughter of an earl, would rather spend her life as a spinster, tending to her garden–alone. But when her father falls critically ill, she suddenly faces the possibility of becoming a penniless relation living on the charity of her sisters unless she can find a husband–now. But facing her fifth Season and feeling unable to meet the requirements of a proper wife, Lily despairs of finding a kind and patient man she can trust enough to marry.

Henry, the war-wounded second son of an earl, needs to have a son to secure his family's future. But worried about his condition worsening and leaving him crippled, he fears turning any future wife into a mere companion and nursemaid. Both are unable to resist the pressure from their families to attend the Season and at least *try* to find a spouse.

Can these two lost causes see past their own limitations and let love in?

ABOUT THE AUTHOR

Daphne Bloom is an author of romances and cozy mysteries. She lives in a quaint Southern town with her family that lets her imagination run free. When she's not watching the latest historical drama on TV, she's usually curled up with her dog and a good book. You can join her newsletter on her website, DaphneBloom.com or follow her on social media.

facebook.com/daphnebloomauthor
instagram.com/daphnebloomauthor
goodreads.com/daphnebloom
bookbub.com/profile/daphne-bloom
tiktok.com/@daphnebloomauthor